DADDY'S Addiction

BJAlpha

Daddy's Addiction

Mistaken identity has never been so wrong.

Tommy

After years of sabotaging my body and blaming my family for the loss of my love, I've refused to be a part of our Mafia involvement.

Then my usual Indulgence service arrives, and for the first time in years, my body comes alive. I can feel.

The only problem is the girl in my arms. The one I crave is not the girl I ordered.

No, it's my stepdaughter.

And worse, she wants me to be her daddy.

I've swapped one addiction for the other, but this one might just be my cure.

Dedication

To all you good little girls who love their men to be possessive, filthy and a tad bit unhinged.
This book is for you.

WARNING

*This is not a light-hearted, sweet and innocent love story.
It is dark and delicious.
It is filthy with a cherry on the top, known as a huge red flag.*

*You're going to need to charge your toys. Have your partner
at hand. Because Daddy Tommy is about to get you very
messy. In the best kind of way.*

Content Warning

This book is intended for adults only.

It contains scenes of violence and graphic sex. Please check my website for a full list of triggers.

Chapter One

Tommy

My head pounds, my temple pulsates, and my body aches like a bitch.

Jesus, what the fuck did I do last night?

Groaning, I roll over and inhale a mouthful of something furry. I splutter in panic when I begin to choke, sitting up, startled. *What the fuck?* I pick strings of hair from my mouth with a grimace and realize one of the whores from last night must have lost a bunch of hair during our rampant sex session.

I probably face fucked her too hard.

My head lolls from side to side as I struggle to focus on anything as the room spins around me. Squeezing my eyes closed, I take a deep breath to compose myself and try to open my eyes once again.

Squinting through narrowed eyes, I'm finally able to take in the destruction of my bedroom. Shit got messy, that's for sure.

Bottles litter the floor, clothes are spewed around, used

condoms are disposed of on every surface, and, for some reason, the large freestanding mirror is laid flat on the floor with remnants of white powder coating it. *Shit.*

I drag a hand through my wayward hair. *I'm such a fucking screwup.*

Scanning the mirror, I take in the pink suctioned dildo still attached to it, and all of a sudden, flashbacks of the previous night come to me, hitting me like a truck from out of nowhere.

Two blondes kiss one another while I relentlessly fuck one from behind and the other bounces up and down, fucking the plastic cock stuck to the mirror. Their moans fill the room while I try in desperation to chase the high and get off—to no avail, as always.

As filthy and depraved as the hookers are, for some reason, I always struggle to finish.

I snort cocaine off their tits and make them lick one another clean.

My stomach clenches in disappointment with myself. What a fucking loser.

Something moves beside me, snapping me out of my memories, and when that something moves toward my cock, I drop back down against the mattress and allow her to slide me into her pouty mouth. Another girl angles herself over me, and her inflated tits hang near my face as her lips come toward mine. "I told you no kissing," I chastise while squeezing her nipple punishingly, forcing her to moan so loud I'm convinced it's fake. "Filthy bitch," I admonish with a half-assed fake smirk. She giggles, but her happiness does nothing for me, nor does the sucking noise from my father's secretary Jenna, as she attempts to shove my cock all the way down her throat but fails miserably and, in turn, leaves a sloppy mess on my stomach that is anything but erotic.

Why can I not feel something? Any-fucking-thing.

The buzzing from my nightstand makes me clench my jaw in irritation as I try my best to remain hard in her mouth.

The noise continues, forcing me to grab my phone, place it down beside me on the mattress, and deliberately put it on loudspeaker, knowing who is calling.

"Tommy?"

I pinch the bridge of my nose at the sound of my father's demanding voice, and his tone is as pissed as ever.

"Tommy?" He tries again when I fail to greet him.

The blonde not sucking me off kisses down the column of my neck, and it feels like insects are crawling over me, trying to burrow beneath my skin. Instead of relaxing me, instead of helping me to get off, all I want is for her to stop. For both of them to stop.

Jesus, I need another hit.

Something to numb my feelings.

"Tommy!" he barks, filling the room and forcing both girls' heads to dart up and glare in the phone's direction.

I grind my teeth. How the fuck dare he take what little pleasure I have away from me? Once again trying to ruin my life.

"What?!" I grind out.

"I want to see you in my office. You have one hour to get there." My chest rises in anger at him intruding on my life. "And get rid of the whores," he tacks on the end before disconnecting the call without another word, reminding me how little importance I am to him anymore. To anyone.

I drop my head back against the pillow with a heavy groan.

Of course, the man knows each and every fucking move

I make. I'm thirty-one years old and my father still tracks me like a goddamn child.

I wonder if he realizes the whore he was referring to is none other than his favorite secretary? I smirk in delight at the thought of pissing him off. Maybe I should tell him? See how much he likes having something so important to him taken away.

"Hurry the fuck up and get me off. I have shit to do," I snap out to the women like the bastard I am. Closing my eyes, I imagine it's her sucking me off, the woman I've spent my life reminiscing about. The only woman I could ever consider settling down with. The only woman I ever kissed and the only woman I will ever give my heart to.

The one they took away from me.

I rest my arms on the back of the office couch. Aggravation builds at the thought of being here when I could be at home in bed with two women getting my cock serviced. My body craves the buzz sex can sometimes give me. It takes the edge off the urge I have to lose myself completely to drugs.

My father's nose turns up, his lip curls in disgust, and his eyes travel up and down my body as if he can see every dirty little detail that ensued last night. I fidget under his scrutiny, tugging on the collar of my shirt as heat travels over me and perspiration gathers on my forehead, yet my mouth is drier than the desert.

"Are you withdrawing again?" He sighs condescendingly, with disapproval lacing his tone.

My eyes lock with his. "No. I told you I only do it recreationally now."

"Mmm." He muses, clucking his tongue like he doesn't believe a single word I utter. He takes a while to finally drag a calculated finger over his lip as he appraises me.

I'll never be good enough in my father's eyes. Not unless I become one of them. Even after I married Zenya to help with my father's business, I wasn't good enough.

"I have to go away on business." He sighs again.

I don't know why he's telling me this—he never normally bothers. So, instead of giving him my attention, I glance away, uninterested in his business, and he knows it. The whole point of my marrying Zenya was for them to leave me the hell alone with my inheritance, and still, they wanted more. They took me for a fool. I should have known then and there that there would be more stipulations in order for me to receive it. The assholes expected me to provide them an heir, no less. I scoff at the memory. As fucking if.

"Zenya's daughter is due to stay with me," he adds, and I face him in confusion. "She's home from boarding school for the holidays." His tone almost sounds sad at the fact he will not be around to see her.

I roll my eyes. Trust my father to have more compassion for someone non-blood-related rather than his own flesh and blood.

"What's this got to do with me?" I sound like a callous bastard, and, well, I am one. But why should I care about her kid? Especially since the bastards didn't even inform me she had one. Where my brothers got their virginal brides, I got a widow with an expenditure. She's damaged goods. Like me, I guess.

"She'll be staying with you." He glares at me.

My spine snaps straight as I sit forward, and my jaw locks as I barely manage to hide the fury bubbling through me. "Over my dead fucking body!" I spit with venom.

He holds his hand up to stop me from going further, as though I'm nothing more than a trained dog.

I know better than to argue with him. I've seen the wrath of my father. I know his ability and the lengths he can go to to get what he wants. If not through violence, then manipulation. My fists clench at my sides, and my body vibrates with anger at him intruding on my life a-fucking-gain.

"She will be staying with you." He stares into my eyes with certainty. The same dark eyes as mine—soulless, dead.

Like mine.

My lips move to argue without thinking. "What about the others? Can't she stay with one of them instead?"

My father's mouth falls open and his eyebrows shoot up in shock. "Your brothers work, Tommy. They have their own responsibilities, and you have yours." His eyes never leave mine.

"She's not my fucking responsibility," I snarl back. "I didn't even know about her until after Zenya died. I don't even know the kid. Nor do I want to," I grit out, then clench my lips shut tight, trying to refrain from going further.

He exhales heavily, unable to hide his disappointment. "Jade. Her name's Jade. And you'll look after her like she's your own." He raises an eyebrow, and his tone leaves no room for discussion.

Shocked, I make an obnoxious choking noise in the back of my throat. The only woman I wanted a child with is long gone, and I sure as hell don't want some other fucker's kid hanging around me. Just because he has a soft spot for the Little Orphan Annie doesn't mean I do.

Ever since Zenya passed away six years ago, my father

has taken that kid in and been a better parent to her than he ever was to any of us. I made a point of avoiding his place at the best of times, so it was easy to stay away from the kid who, by law, is, in fact, my legal responsibility. Just another thing they fucked me over with. I grind my teeth at the reminder of the injustice.

Until now, my father has asked nothing from me where the girl is concerned, so I've never asked about her in return. Why would I? I live my life and they live theirs.

"How long will you be gone?"

"Six weeks."

"Six?" I question in outrage, and my jaw drops open. "Six fucking weeks?"

"Tommy, if you want to continue the lifestyle you have, I suggest you put it on hold for six weeks. That's all I ask." He smooths his palms down his shirt as though he's finished with the conversation.

I slump back in my chair. He's punishing me all over again. The hold he has over me is money. Without him, I have none and he knows it. And boy, do I fucking know it.

Dragging my hand through my hair, I try to come up with a plan. Maybe I can get her a nanny or something? A sitter? I can ask my housekeeper to arrange it.

Yes, yes, I'll do that. I'll get someone to amuse the kid while I live my life. I can handle six weeks. I can continue living my life while the kid is cared for. Nothing needs to change.

"I need her in a safe environment," he adds on, as if reading my thoughts.

He doesn't mean her living with me as a form of protection because that goes without saying. As a Mafia family, we're all protected. No, he's referring to my lifestyle choices. The drugs, drinking, and sex.

"I mean it, Tommy. No drugs. Six fucking weeks, that's all I ask."

Huh, like it's that easy.

"Fine," I snap out. "When does she arrive?" I stand and head toward the door, finished with the conversation.

"Saturday," he calls out as I walk through it, but I don't miss the sound of hope in his voice, making me want to vomit at the pathetic notion.

"Look after her." His words barely register.

Chapter Two

Tommy

I've been angsty as fuck all week, and I'm ready to blow off some steam. So when the doorbell rings, signaling my Saturday night Indulgence girl, I race down the stairs like the addict I am, ready for my next hit.

Glancing at the mirror at the bottom of the stairs, I grin to myself. I was blessed with looks, that's for sure. At least the whores I fuck get to screw someone good-looking. I swing open the front door eagerly to find a young woman staring up at me with wide green eyes full of uncertainty. Scanning over her, I take in her bedraggled state, she's drenched, and the thought pisses me off that the car clearly didn't drop her at the door like usual. The rain lashes down behind her and she shivers, making my eyes latch on to her outfit of choice for tonight.

The girl opted for a school uniform. My lip quirks up in delight. This is new, different, and my cock is on board with it as it pulsates and springs to life from a mere glance at her. My balls tighten, drawing up with need, especially when my gaze roams over her trembling lips and her peaked nipples begging to be sucked and toyed with. I graze a hand over my solid cock, letting her know how much I approve of her outfit. Her eyes widen innocently. Fuck me, she's adorable and edible all rolled into one. I'm going to have some fun with her. It's been a long time since my cock had this reaction to a woman—years.

My mouth waters to taste her, and my cock leaks to devour her and fill her until I spill down her thighs. Fuck yes.

Her soaked hair sticks to her face as loose brunette waves trail down her shoulders and over the fabric of her white school shirt, which clings to her, making it see-through thanks to the heavy downpour. And fuck my life am I grateful for it. Her tits strain the buttons, and those pebbled nipples are the perfect size, ready to tug into my mouth, nibble and caress, mark as mine.

A pleated school skirt reaches her midthigh, and I itch to push it up around her waist while dropping to my knees and honoring the little siren sent to torture me with impure thoughts.

Fuck, Indulgence outdid themselves this time. I need to shoot the owner, Oscar O'Connell, a thank-you message. My lip tips up at the thought.

My hand snaps out and I grab her wrist forcefully, causing a small gasp of surprise to leave her plump lips. That little murmur alone sends a bolt of electricity through my body, bringing me to life while making my cock leak strings of precum from the tip, marking my pants in the process. Never have I had such a reaction to a simple touch.

Tugging her inside, I spin her to face me and slam her against the wall. "Tsk, tsk, naughty little girl, dressing like this." My gaze travels over her body, and she sucks in a sharp breath, then nibbles on her bottom lip under the intensity of my stare. "You look like a little whore." I push myself against her, my solid cock flush against her small frame. "Such a naughty little girl." Gently, I allow my thumb to graze her bottom lip, my voice a gentle whisper against her smooth skin, "You're making me hard, little girl." Her green eyes bulge, and her lips part, giving me the perfect opportunity to slam my mouth against hers without thinking. I shove my tongue deep inside her mouth with a growl. My hand entwines with her hair, fisting it hard, and I tug it back so sharply she winces with the bite of pain behind my action. Her small hands try to shove me away, but it only makes me press against her harder, enjoying this little push-pull game she's playing with me. She makes me smile into the kiss when her hands grip my shirt instead of forcing me away, giving up on the fight as quickly as starting it. I like her submissive against me. Revel in it even.

My pulse races as heat spreads through my body, and a fierce determination to fuck her ruthlessly drives me wild, feral, with a need to claim her. Roughly, I grind my solid cock against her petite frame again, earning a whimper that I swallow whole as my grip on her hair tightens and so does her body.

Pulling back breathlessly to stare at her with our chests rising in unison, I realize I've actually kissed the girl. My lips tingle, my heart hammers and my mouth goes dry as our eyes remain locked. Of course, she has no idea of the enormity of the situation, but I do.

This little minx is mine.

If only for tonight.

Jade

My heart thuds erratically against my chest. His black eyes are familiar, yet I refuse to acknowledge them. I refuse to believe this man is my stepfather.

He can't be. Can he?

His dark hair is a tousled mess, short on the sides and longer on top. The upper buttons of his white shirt are open, exposing his olive skin—familiar olive skin.

I shake my head, refusing to believe it. Surely not.

His jawline is sharp, chiseled, and his face is stern in a very Mafia way I've become all too familiar with. I shake my head again. It can't be.

He drags his tongue languorously over his lip as if savoring my taste. The action is somehow seductive and makes me squirm as wetness gathers in my panties from the sheer warmth penetrating from his body. His blatant perusal of my body, along with the growing sexual tension between us, has my cheeks heating with embarrassment. "You're the hottest little whore they've ever sent."

I freeze at his words, and my eyes grow wide when he

shoves my skirt up as I effortlessly attempt to tug it back down and register his words.

Something isn't right here. So I try and reason with him. "I think . . ." He kisses my neck and groans against me, making me sigh into him, molding against him like putty. "I think . . ." I try again, but words struggle to form. "I think there's been a mistake," I breathe out in a pathetic whisper when his fingers trail along the fabric of my cotton panties, grazing my throbbing clit. He heaves me up against the wall, and his hard cock throbs against me. I lose any coherent thought under his touch, and when he presses the tips of his fingers harder against my aching bud, I can't help the desperate whimper that slips from my lips, "Please."

A throat clears from behind him, and I jolt, but he ignores the man and continues sucking my neck, making me melt into him with a purr of satisfaction.

I've never felt anything like this before. Sure, I've fooled around with boys, fumbling boys, but this is a man taking what he wants from me.

The throat clears again. "Sir, your guest has arrived." I peer over his shoulder to a man dressed in a butler outfit.

He chuckles against me, pressing a soft kiss to my neck before he drops me to my feet and turns toward the butler. "Yes, obviously, Marshall. Thank you," he grits out, positioning himself in front of me as if not wanting Marshall to see me. The thought of his possessiveness has me craving him even more. I feel wanted for the first time in my life, and I crave more of it.

Marshall clears his throat again and, this time, steps forward.

"What the fuck is it, Marshall? What now?" he snaps, his eyes flaring with rage.

"I'm sorry, sir. It's just your guest is coming up the

driveway now." Marshall glances toward the door, and he turns in that direction. Confusion mars his face, his eyebrows narrow slightly. Marshall steps forward and lowers his voice. "I believe there's been an unfortunate mistake, sir."

There's a knock on the door, making him turn to me, then the door once again.

"I believe this is Miss Jade," Marshall responds while holding his hand out in my direction.

"Miss Jade?" My name rolls off his tongue as he repeats it slowly, and I whimper at the growly edge to it.

I nod frantically like an idiot at Marshall's assumption. Nerves racking through me, but something else too. Need.

His hooded eyes scan over me. "Miss Jade." He repeats, as though unsure of who I am. Surely, they told him I was coming.

Marshall moves forward, lowering his head toward his ear and speaking so low I almost don't hear. Almost.

"Miss Zenya's daughter, sir. Your stepdaughter."

I recognize the moment the words register in his head. His face pales, and his eyes widen in horror, and he steps back so quick it's as though he's been burned.

I close my eyes at the surge of pain that single action causes.

With my lips still tingling from his kiss, my panties still wet from his touch, and my heart still hammering from desire, the disappointment curdles inside me like an infection spreading to my bloodstream.

Tommy drops his head, placing his hands on his hips, and every muscle in his body seems coiled tight as he takes sharp, deep breaths that make my heart race in panic.

The atmosphere turns cold. Dangerous even.

Slowly, he raises his dark gaze toward mine, and his

nostrils flare. His venomous glare has my lip trembling at the sudden turn of events.

"Take her the fuck upstairs and keep her the hell away from me!" he spits in my direction, and my heart plummets in devastation.

Chapter Three

Jade

When Tommy walked away from me, I'd never felt so used and degraded in my entire life. I dropped my head in shame as I followed Marshall up the stairs for him to show me to my room. He's an older gentleman with kind eyes and an even kinder smile. Pity oozed from him, and I couldn't find it in me at that moment to feel mad about it.

But now that I sit in this lavish princess-themed bedroom staring at the pretty pink walls and ridiculously frilly decor, anger is bursting to get out.

How dare he?

How dare he make my body feel alive with the unadulterated lust in his eyes. More alive than I have for the last eighteen years I've been on earth.

Then his touch—oh, wow—and those lips sent a thousand bolts of electricity through my veins and a tsunami to my panties that even my Clit 3000 can't achieve.

And then, when he realized who I was, he turned his

anger with himself into hate toward me. How dare he?

What sort of man opens the door to a girl in a school uniform and assumes she's there for sex, anyway?

I was already out of sorts at being thrust into my stepfather's life when I couldn't even remember meeting him in the first place. If I wasn't so desperate to feel wanted, I'd have stayed at the boarding school, but all my friends had somewhere to go, and I normally look forward to being at Mr. Marino's house during school break.

To say I was disappointed to hear he was rushed away on business is an understatement, and now I'm stuck here, unwanted. Only, for a few minutes, I felt like I was someone's everything.

My mind has been mulling over the events all night long, and I've barely been able to sleep a wink after his touch made me desperate for something I've never felt before. Desperate for him.

He hires prostitutes, I'm sure of it. My nose scrunches up in disgust. His hands touched me when they've also touched them, yet I can't help but feel partial jealousy toward them at how they have experienced more of him than I ever have. Probably ever will, now that he knows who I am.

I sink back into the lacy pink pillow and touch my finger to my lips.

There's no way he's getting away with making me feel like this.

Used.

Sitting up, I straighten my shoulders with renewed vigor.

I'll show Tommy Marino I can be everything his whores can be.

And so, so much more.

Tommy

My cock won't go down. It's stuck up in a perpetual state of shock. Like the damn thing has been electrocuted, and it's so fucking stiff it feels like rigor mortis has set in. But I refuse to acknowledge it, hoping the fucker gets the message sooner or later. Preferably the former.

It chafes against my boxers with each step I take, and as I open the door to the kitchen, it almost leaps out of my jeans at the sight before me.

Jesus fucking Christ. How the hell am I meant to deal with this shit? I grind my jaw from side to side as my entire body tenses in awareness at her proximity.

Her back is to me, but given how her shoulders have tightened, she knows I've walked into the room, and the air changes around us.

I grit my teeth in annoyance while scanning over her perky little ass perched at the breakfast bar like she belongs there. She's in sleep shorts that have me wondering if she's wearing panties beneath them. *Jesus, I'm screwed.*

I scrub a hand over my head and exhale, vowing to get

laid as soon as possible and banish her from my thoughts once and for all.

Making my way toward the refrigerator, I ignore the feel of her eyes on me and take my morning juice out and a fresh Danish pastry from beneath the warmer.

Turning to face her, I manage to hide my hard cock behind the counter. This is not what I want my step-daughter to see. I grimace at the thought, but worse than that, my cock aches at her presence—the element of taboo corrupting the poor fucker.

Her green eyes meet mine, and for a moment, I'm stunned to silence at how beautiful she is. My gaze scrutinizes her. A scattering of freckles covers the top of her nose. Her hair is up in some sort of messy bun, elongating her neck, which has a mark on the side. A mark I'm certain I gave her. The memory causes my throat to go dry and my cock to weep. I cling to the counter to refrain from stroking over it, desperate for some relief—any fucking relief right now.

I've not given anyone a hickey before. Other than Justine, anyway. My jaw clenches at the reminder.

Slowly, my eyes wander down to her lacy camisole top and farther down toward her tits. Jesus. She's not wearing a fucking bra, and my mouth waters at the sight before me. Bringing my drink to my mouth, I try and disguise my need for her, but I can't look away from her tits. Christ, I can even see her darkened nipples, for fuck's sake.

My hand tightens on the juice, and I slam the pastry onto the counter, crushing it beneath my palm as I glance over my shoulder to make sure no staff are around and might have seen her dressed like this. She jumps at my reaction, spilling milk from the spoon down her chest. I watch in rapture as it trickles beneath her top, around the valley of her tits and onto her nipples, no doubt. I groan internally. That beautiful, plush, young flesh that makes my mouth water to sink my teeth into. And fuck, she has the perfect pair of tits to push my cock through as I hold her by her pretty little throat while she panics at the force of me plowing into her hard.

"Daddy?"

My eyes snap up toward hers, and my cock pulsates in my pants, forcing me to grip the counter with both hands again just to stop myself from lunging forward and taking her here and now on the counter.

I choke out my words. "What did you just call me?"

"Daddy." She smirks. "That's who you are, right, my daddy?"

Forcing past the uncomfortable lump in my throat, I clear it and lean over the counter, forcing her confident bravado to lean back away from me. "Don't call me that." I keep my voice dark, deep and full of threat as I stare unwavering into her eyes.

Where I expected her to back down, to show me fear and compliance, I find none. No, the little minx tips her lip up at the side and continues to eat her cereal like she didn't make me almost come in my pants at how she addressed me.

"I want my room changed." She places another spoonful of cereal in her mouth, and I watch the motion, entranced by her tongue flicking out, and am jealous of the drop of milk she seizes and draws back into her small mouth. Fuck, my cum would look sensational pumping out of her lips and down toward those plush tits.

"You clearly thought I was a child." She smiles now and holds her head high while pointing the spoon in my direction. "As you can see. I'm not."

My gaze once again roams over her body. She's not a fucking child; she's anything but.

Mentally chastising myself, I quickly snap my gaze back up to hers and refuse to glance down toward her sensational tits. "What's wrong with your room?"

Her nose scrunches, making her look adorable. *Since when the fuck do I consider someone adorable?*

Her eyebrows shoot up, and her mouth falls open in horror. "Have you seen it?"

"No."

She blows out a deep breath I feel all the way to my balls. I wonder what it would feel like having that pouty little mouth around them? Her heavy pants against me while I fill her naughty mouth and make her cry while I stuff her. I smirk at the thought. That would show her who's in charge. Her fucking daddy!

"It's hideous. Who decorated it?"

My mind tries to play catch-up with what she's saying as I tell myself not to consider her mouth anywhere near my balls.

"My father's secretary."

"She needs to be informed that I'm eighteen, not eight," she spits while eating her cereal, causing bits to fall from her mouth. *Did nobody teach her not to speak with her mouth full?*

"No. Actually, they didn't. My real dad is dead, and my mom is too. But you know that already, don't you, Daddy?"

I hadn't realized I said the words out loud. I ignore her calling me Daddy. Something tells me she's having far too much fun addressing me with the term and is using it more as a form of punishment than an endearment.

"You need to wear more clothes around the house,

Jade." Her name rolls off my tongue as smooth as butter and as sweet as honey.

She rolls back slightly in her chair, feigning shock. "So do you." She counters with a flick of her spoon in my direction. I glance down at my bare chest. It wasn't intentional to walk around in just my jeans this morning, though I do not do it regularly, so maybe it was. "Maybe I should go bare-chested like you?" She smiles cunningly.

A low growl emits from me, and I lean over the counter, and she slinks farther back. "Put some fucking clothes on before I fucking force you."

"Make me!" She glares at me with fire in her eyes.

The thought of punishing her disrespect has my balls drawing up. Anger boils inside me at my reaction toward her. How has my body become so desperate for her, and she hasn't even been here twenty-four hours yet?

I lean over the counter, narrowing my eyes, and give in to the darkness inside of me. "Get. Some. Fucking. Clothes. On. Before. I. Spank. You. So. Fucking. Hard. You. Won't. Sit. Down. For. A. Fucking. Week!"

She shudders at the deep tone of my voice, the menace behind it emphasizing the promise of my words. I smile with pride at her shocked response. The way her shoulders slump, her smooth skin pales, and her lip trembles. Fuck, I like her scared and fragile. Easy for me to break and pleasurable to piece back together.

Silently, she slides off the chair, and I'm torn between being relieved or disappointed at her leaving.

For the first time in as long as I can remember, I feel something other than the mundane emptiness I normally feel.

I feel alive.

But then she stops in the doorway, turns her head over

her shoulder, and gifts me with a soft smile. "Yes, Daddy." She sashays out of the room, taking my balls with her and leaving my mouth agape.

I flick the lid off my juice and guzzle it down with only one thought.

How in the hell am I not going to fuck my stepdaughter?

Chapter Four

Jade

A loud giggle interrupts my thoughts and freezes my blood. I flick off the television and throw the remote on the lacy pink bedding, grimacing at the abomination of prettiness. Moving toward my bedroom door, the high-pitched noise becomes louder, grating on my nerves. Did he bring a woman back here? When only last night he was going to fuck me against the wall.

He's an animal, albeit a gorgeous one.

My fists tighten at his blatant disregard for my feelings. Does he feel anything for me at all? Or was I just another fuck toy, like all the other women he uses for his needs? How can he easily discard me for another body to empty his load into? Jealousy flows through me and I curl my lip in disgust as I tear open the bedroom door. My feet slap against the tiles of the spiral staircase as I storm toward the living area.

My gorgeous stepfather sits on the couch with his arms

draped along the back, and his hand tightens around his glass as I approach.

Tommy's legs are stretched out wide and his white shirt is open, showcasing his tattooed skin. Skin I want to drag my tongue over and explore. He makes me feel things I've never felt before.

The blonde beside him roams her hand up and down his chiseled body, making me want to tear her talons from her fingers.

When she turns to face me, I almost choke. She's the complete opposite of me, and again, inadequacy races through my body at lightning speed.

"Who are you?" I ask, giving her my full attention and ignoring Tommy altogether. I hate myself for sounding so vulnerable in this moment, but I lift my chin and cross my arms over my chest, allowing the anger to take over.

She nuzzles against his neck and acts as though I'm not even there. Like I'm insignificant. Tommy's lip lifts at the side. He loves making me feel insignificant like everyone else in my life does.

God, he makes me want to slap him across his handsome face.

Instead of wavering under their scrutiny, I stand taller. I have spent my entire life in boarding school and dealt with my fair share of bullies. I know how to handle them just fine.

When the blonde doesn't respond, I turn my attention toward Tommy, ignoring the woman. "Do you know this one's name?" I tilt my head in her direction, and the blonde sucks in a sharp disgruntled noise of surprise while raising her head from his neck. Her eyes flick from me to Tommy and back again.

"The one last night didn't last very long, did she?" I

grind out, letting him know how pissed I am with how easily he disposed of me.

He works his jaw from side to side as if he's thinking of a sharp comeback. Then his eyes latch on to mine. "She was far too inexperienced for me." His lips twitch, and I narrow my eyes on him.

My heart hammers in my chest and my mind whirls with his words as I curl my fingers into fists at my side. He doesn't miss the action either and slowly raises his glass to his lips, but not before giving me a mock salute with it—all while his bimbo's eyes ping-pong between us.

I seethe with internal rage. The bastard. He watches me closely, expecting me to give in and stomp away like a child.

Well, fuck him, and fuck her too.

I narrow my eyes and raise my chin. "My daddy tried to fuck me last night," I snipe out and drop my eyes to the blonde, whose mouth gapes open. "And now he's saying he doesn't want me because I'm too inexperienced." I wobble my lip ever so slightly, just enough for it to warrant a look of hurt.

My time in boarding school helped me learn techniques to stay alive among a pack of ravenous wolves who rip apart the weak.

Weak, I am not.

Tommy chokes on his drink, and the blonde pulls away from him with a look of disgust marring her plastic features. A smile itches to form on my lips, but I force it back and straighten my lips into a scowl. But when Tommy slams his drink onto the table in front of him and jumps to his feet with his face contorted in anger, I second-guess my actions. Maybe I went too far.

He lunges for me and grabs me so roughly by the arm he'll leave marks, then drags me from the room, and heat radiates from him as his chest heaves uncontrollably. His grip tightens further when my bare feet slide across the marble floor reluctantly, my toes curl into the marble in a lame attempt to stop our movements. "I'm sorry," I whine, realizing I've gone too far.

"Sorry?" he spits as he bends down and picks me up, then throws me over his shoulder to quicken the pace.

He strides up the stairs two at a time and swings open my bedroom door before dropping me on my bed, and I bounce from the abrupt force.

Exhaling loudly, he steps back.

Then his eyes roam over the room, and his lip curls up in disapproval. "What the actual fuck?"

I sit up on my elbows. "I know, right?"

His dark eyes latch on to me, and my heart thuds louder with each second ticking by, and when he takes in my open bare legs, I lick my lips in anticipation.

Tommy's hands move lightning fast, gripping my ankles, and he tugs me toward the edge of the bed before lowering himself. He grips my throat, pulling me off the mattress toward him as he looms over my small body, dark eyes drilling into me, danger lurking beneath them.

He's so close I can smell the alcohol on his breath, see a scar on his lip and almost touch them with mine.

My clit throbs with the awareness, and my body becomes putty in his hands, waiting with expectation and need. "I don't need some little girl in my life flirting with me." His eyes roam over me in distaste, making my lip tremble in hurt.

He applies pressure to my throat, my eyes widen and my pulse races in panic. "Don't test me, little girl. Stay the hell away from me. You don't know what I'm capable of," he spits out with spite. In a move I couldn't anticipate, he pushes me back by my throat until my body collides with the soft sheets. "I like to break things, little girl." His pupils have dilated, and the threat behind his words lies heavy in the air. "Break them and destroy them. Don't push me. You won't be repairable if you do." With that threat, he finally releases me and leaves me gasping for air and my clit begging for a release I swear only he can give.

My body droops in defeat as Tommy Marino turns and walks briskly out of my room.

He might think he scared me into submission, but my panties are proof otherwise.

No, dangerous Tommy turns me on.

He will be a challenge, but I like nothing more than a challenge, and judging by that solid cock of his, he likes one too.

Tommy

I leave Jade's room and storm downstairs and guzzle the remainder of the scotch from the bottle. When nails begin to graze my neckline, I grimace at the prickly sensation they leave in their wake. I'd forgotten I ordered company for tonight.

I snap and tell her to leave and then follow it up with a text to my security, who escorts her off the property. My cock is so hard it throbs against the band of my boxers, aching with a desperate need to punish her little pussy. My little girl's pussy. Fuck me, that's wrong. But feels so fucking right.

Now I'm lying in bed with a raging hard-on I can't neglect any longer.

Taking a deep breath, I tug down my boxers and pull out my rock-hard cock. It's angry and aches, all thanks to the little cocktease across the hall. I have a good mind to go into her room, pull the sheet from her perfect little body, and force my cock into her mouth until she chokes on it for so long her throat becomes raw.

Fisting my cock in a steel grip, I slowly swipe the dripping head with my thumb and coat myself in the excessive precum leaking from the tip and work my hand up and down my cock in a tight fist.

Tormenting myself, I imagine it's her small mouth that I'm feeding, and the pulsating vein on my cock encourages my thoughts deeper. I close my eyes and imagine the scenario taking place. How her eyes would bulge with shock at the size of me in comparison to her small frame. How I'd hold her throat roughly and not stop fucking it until it's ragged and raw, forcing her to take all of me. Tears would spill from her eyes, dribble would flow down her chin, and she'd choke on my cum as I spilled into her mouth. Then I'd pull out while she gasped for air, and I'd wipe my cock clean on her innocent cheeks and make her suck the excess cum from me.

Thrusting my hips up, I lower my free hand to my balls and tug on them. Pleasure rushes through my body as I imagine painting her lips with my cum while she begs me for more. My body tightens as I fuck my palm harder, and my breathing becomes ragged as the blood pumps furiously through my veins. She's being a desperate, needy little whore for me to use as I please. My cock leaks over my hand. "Fuck yes, you little slut." My muscles tense when cum shoots from my cock as I continue to fist it in a firm grip. "Fuck, little girl. Fuck," I pant out as my breath quickens.

It lands on my stomach and coats my thighs. "Fuck, little girl. All for you. Daddy came all for you."

My chest heaves as I stare down at my abs coated in my thick cum and use the tip of my finger to write her name on my stomach. Then I rub my cock with the palm of my hand as I stiffen once again.

I should make the little whore clean it up.
And I will.
One day, I'll make her pay for making me feel this way.

Chapter Five

Jade

I blow into my hot chocolate while Ellie grins over at Darryl. "So, are you working Friday?" he asks me, unaware my best friend is majorly crushing on him right now.

Sure, he's a good-looking guy, but I'm not looking for a boy. He does nothing for me, not like Tommy. Even his name makes me want to drop to my knees and beg him to take me. *Tommy Marino, mmm.*

"Jade. I said, are you working Friday?" He snaps me out of my daydream.

"No. Just the weekend."

His brown eyes flare with hope as he sits forward on the picnic bench. "We could come to your place." He throws his arm out toward the guys playing basketball.

I groan inside and rub my temple at the thought of having a group of people over at the mansion.

"Come on, Jade. We've never been to yours." He whines, his eyes imploring mine with hope.

I scoff. "Yeah, there's a reason for that. I don't have a home, remember?" A pang of hurt hits me square in the chest, but I quickly shake it off, as usual.

Darryl's eyes fill with sympathy, but it's gone just as quick. "Right. Orphan, got it." He taps the table, and Ellie's and my eyes bug out at his nonchalant words. "Well, you said you're living with your stepfather this summer, right?"

My heart races, my stomach flips with butterflies, and heat flushes over me at the mention of Tommy. I give him a small nod, hoping he can't see the need I have inside me for my stepfather bursting to get out.

"So we can just party there." He shrugs like it's nothing.

I chew on my lip with uncertainty. Unlike all my friends, I've not had a party before, nor had friends over.

But why shouldn't I have some fun? He has fun.

Tommy told me to stay out of his way, shrugging me off like some inconvenience. Maybe it's time I became the teenager he expects me to be.

"What were you thinking exactly?" I ask, and he grins like a Cheshire cat.

"Pool, beers, skimpy bikinis." He smiles while doing a weird dance with his eyebrows. Ellie bursts out laughing, then slaps at his arm in a playful move, but it's obviously flirty; she practically has hearts in her eyes whenever Darryl is around.

"Okay." I nod. Excitement builds inside me. "I can do this."

The table breaks out into a chorus of "Oh yeah" and "Bring it on" while my mind considers which bikini is the skimpiest I own.

I'll show my stepfather what a little girl can look like. I smirk to myself as I take another sip of my hot chocolate while my plan comes together.

He's going to wonder what the hell hit him.

The music is so loud I'm sure the next town over can hear it. Darryl looks hot in his board shorts with his bronzed chest on display. As if he senses my gaze, his eyes lock with mine, and he says something to one of his friends before nodding and bringing the beer bottle to his lips. His Adam's apple bobs in his throat as he swallows.

"Jesus, he's so hot." Ellie groans beside me as I lather another layer of sunscreen onto my shoulders.

"He is."

"I knew it!" She bounces up and down on her feet, making me giggle at her response. "Seriously, Jade, as much as I'd like to suck face with that hottie"—she throws her thumb over her shoulder—"it's obvious he's into you. I say go for it."

I chew on my lip as I assess Darryl.

Staring off toward the pool, my mind wanders to how Tommy would feel seeing me have a good time with him.

A shadow covers me, and I dart my eyes up to see Darryl grinning down at me. "Fancy a game of volleyball?" He drags a hand through his wet hair. "You can sit on my shoulders." He smirks, and I smile back at him.

He leans down and offers his hand, but unlike when my skin touches Tommy's, no goose bumps travel over me and there're no tingles of excitement as I slip my palm into his. I know the only man I want to touch me is my daddy, and I can't wait for him to see me play.

Tommy

Loud music wakes me, and for a moment, I forget where I am. My head pulsates with each beat, and I groan in irritation. As I get to my feet, my head spins, and I kick an empty bottle across my bedroom floor. I ignore the thudding vibrations from outside and opt for a piss and then shower to freshen up.

Flicking on the jets, I step into the warm water. My head falls back as I relish in the heat flowing down my body, washing away my heavy head and cleansing my body of the sins from last night.

There's no denying the way I feel toward my stepdaughter, as my constant solid cock is a reminder in itself. Staring down at it, my fingers twitch to relieve it once again.

Fuck, I bet her lips would feel sensational wrapped around the head, suckling on it like the good little girl I know she can be. Precum leaks from the tip, and yet again, I give in to the overwhelming urge to pleasure myself. I work my cock faster and faster, punishingly in my fist, my balls draw up and with her name dripping from my lips, I slam my palm against the tiles and come with a roar that makes my head fall forward.

Switching off the shower, I step out and towel off. I've completely forgotten about the disturbance happening outside until the floorboards vibrate beneath my feet.

What in the fuck is she doing?

I storm into the bedroom and pull open the dresser drawer, then tug on some shorts, grab my sunglasses to cover my sensitive eyes, and make my way downstairs with fire in my veins.

Shouts and giggles filter through the foyer as I follow the sounds of a party. *What the fuck does she think she's playing at?*

Rage fills me as I storm through my kitchen and throw open the patio doors to find at least a dozen young people in my swimming pool.

What the hell?

Anger boils inside me, forcing my jaw to clench tight as I scan the pool for my stepdaughter.

I lift my sunglasses to locate my daughter and throw them onto the patio table as I step toward the pool.

The moment my eyes land on her, a fire like never before consumes me. My shoulders tense, my hands ball into fists, and my veins fill with jealous possession.

She's on some prick's shoulders, hitting a ball to an opponent, and her tits bounce as she does. The red scrap of a bikini barely covers her ass cheeks where he holds her—fucking holds her!

His flesh is against hers as she clings to the little prick's head and smiles down at him.

My temper skyrockets, threatening to destroy every fucker in my path.

"Jade!" I roar across the pool and above the music. Every head turns in my direction.

Her mouth falls open in shock as she taps the guy's shoulder for him to lower her into the water. He smirks at her when she says something, and then the little prick with a death wish bends and whispers something in her ear that makes her freeze.

What the hell did he say to her?

Are they dating?

Is she fucking him?

Without giving her the opportunity to second-guess her move, and with her eyes locked onto mine, I point at the floor in front of me, commanding her to vacate the pool. "Now!" I bellow when she doesn't move quick enough.

Slowly, like a fucking goddess, she wades through the water toward me. Each step makes my heart hammer and my cock jump, greedy for her.

The little prick stares at her ass cheeks as she sways toward me. My heart leaps in my chest at her beauty. And when my eyes dart back up toward the little prick, he licks his lips, with his eyes zoned in on my little girl's ass. Over my dead fucking body, motherfucker. Nobody will touch her. Nobody but me.

When she's within arm's reach, my hand snaps out and tugs her up the steps, making her stumble against my rigid chest.

"Tommy?"

"Save it," I snipe out and march us through the house toward my office.

"I'm dripping everywhere, Tommy." Her voice comes out panicked and laced with concern, but I ignore her.

Dripping? My cock is fucking dripping. It twitches as I replay her words.

Her wet, soft skin in my hand is an aphrodisiac I could do without.

Pushing open the door, I tug her inside and kick it shut behind me before heading straight for my desk. Without giving her time to consider what might happen, I spin her to face the desk and push my hand against her spine, forcing her chest against the wood. Her almost bare ass is exposed, begging for the taking. She tries to push herself up, but I hold her down with ease as she claws at the woodwork. The excitement behind her struggle makes my veins fill with an insatiable need for her. "Tommy, I'm sorry."

I cluck my tongue. "Oh, no. No, you don't, little girl. There's no calling me Tommy now."

With my free hand, I push her bikini panties into the crook of her ass and revel in the goose bumps spreading over her delicate skin at my touch. I palm a perfect globe, squeezing it hard for emphasis, reminding her who is in control here. My granite-hard cock strains against my shorts, pushing through the waistband, determined to be released and get in on the action as it weeps at our contact.

I raise my hand high, then bring it down hard against her ass cheek, delighting in the whoosh of air to leave her stunned lips. A reddened mark is left in my wake, and I revel in it.

"Apologize. Say, 'Sorry, Daddy, for being a slut.'"

"Oh my god," she mumbles, then slams her eyes closed when my palm strikes her ass again. With each touch of her skin, my balls tighten with desire.

"I'm . . ." *Smack.* My chest rises with excitement.

"Sorry . . ." *Smack.* The need to drive my cock inside her makes me desperate to hear her pleas.

"Daddy . . ." *Smack.* Fuck, she's incredible.

"For being—" She snivels. "A slut." *Smack.*

My palm burns and her ass reddens further as her sobs fill the room. Triumph fills me, along with desire flooding my veins at her punishment. Fuck, she's incredible, and the fact she took her punishment so well for me fills me with pride. The sudden need to reassure her overwhelms me. Not something I'm used to when toying with my nightly whores.

"Good girl." I gently palm her hot flesh, and she practically mews at the contact. "Such a good girl for taking your punishment." She sniffles, and I release her, allowing her to stand to her full height on trembling legs. I untuck her bikini from her ass and gently place it back over her reddened globes. Then I drape the hair from off her shoulder, pushing it to one side before placing a gentle kiss on the curve of her neck. A whimper escapes her lips, forcing me to cup her chin between my forefingers. Then I ease my thumb into her mouth.

"Suck it like a good girl." She does as I command, and when her wet tongue flicks over my thumb, I allow myself to gift her. "Let Daddy reward you."

Her body tenses, but she allows me to slip my hand below her waistline. "Such a needy little girl for Daddy's touch." I breathe against her ear as I place kisses along her neck while trailing my fingers over her soft, bare mound. I groan at the contact with her flesh, and when I graze her clit, a delicate moan escapes her, and my heart races as my balls pull tight with eagerness.

Lowering my head, I breathe against her ear. "Grind against Daddy's hand," I encourage.

With her back against me, my thumb in her mouth, and her body flush against the desk, she rocks her ass back and forth against my solid cock while allowing me to rub her clit.

"Can you feel how hard Daddy's cock is?" I pant while swirling my two fingers around her wet pussy.

"Mmm." She flicks her tongue over my thumb, and my eyes roll in ecstasy.

"Are you going to let Daddy in your little pussy hole, little girl?"

"Mmm." She sucks harder, making me hiss through my teeth, and my cock pulsates. I punish her by clamping my teeth ruthlessly into her neck, tugging her soft skin and pulling it sharply to mark her.

"Little fucking whore," I grind out, rubbing her swollen bud faster and faster.

Touching her makes me feel a burning fire of passion deep inside. A possession like no other rolls through me. She's fucking mine. Mine to corrupt. Mine to keep and protect. All fucking mine.

"Ohhh." She rocks faster against my solid cock, her orgasm approaching.

"That's it. Keep sucking. Imagine it's Daddy's cock you're milking for him like a good girl." I flick my fingers over her swollen clit and press down after gifting it with a circular motion, then I repeat the action.

"Oh god."

Her body tightens, and my thumb slips from her mouth as her lips fall open, like when I imagined my cock falling from her before spraying her innocent face with my cum.

"Daddy!" She moans against me as her head falls back against my chest where I hold her throat so tight I will leave marks, and our eyes lock as she comes. Our breaths are escalated, and the moment feels euphoric as my fingertips dig into her flesh.

Not giving her a chance to come down from her orgasm, I spin her around and push her to her knees. Her dazed eyes barely register the action as I pull my cock from my shorts and fist myself over her shell-shocked face.

Her wide eyes make me smirk. Using the same thumb she sucked into her mouth, I tug her mouth wider, holding it there as my balls draw up. "Fuck, yes!" I fire my pleasure over her face as I stare down at the ropes of my warm, thick cum landing in her mouth, coating her lips, and painting her cheeks.

"Fuck, little girl."

My body slowly comes down from the most incredible orgasm that's ever ripped from me. And just like in my dreams, I wipe the tip of my wet cock down her cheek before sliding it into her mouth, where she sucks it clean with her tongue, suckling the tender head and making my eyes roll to the back of my head on a growl.

Finally, with my cock twitching, I bring my gaze back to hers, and her eyes flash with a look of vulnerability, and that look alone sends a surge of protective need through me. Grazing the back of my hand down her cheek, I reassure her. "Such a good girl for Daddy."

She gifts me with a nod, and her lips tip into a smile when I slide from her mouth and tuck myself back into my shorts. A smile that warms a part of me I thought was dead. And for the first time in years, I find myself smiling too.

Chapter Six

Tommy

She's been gone all fucking day, and I have no idea where the hell she is. Why the fuck didn't I put a tracker on her phone?

I throw down my pen because I can't concentrate on a single thing.

As far as my father knows, I don't work, but he doesn't know I keep track of the nightclub accounts and feed the information back to Rafael, as I refuse to allow my father the knowledge of me accepting any Mafia responsibility.

Of course, Rafael keeps it quiet because this is all shit he should be doing, but I actually enjoy keeping my mind active. Though I continue to allow my father to think the worst of me, I let him believe I do nothing with my time other than fulfill my drug and sex addictions. Whatever I do won't be good enough in his eyes, so why try and prove otherwise? I do this for me, not him.

But today, my mind isn't on work. No, it's stuck on the

girl that came storming into my life like a fucking whirlwind.

She might be my stepdaughter, but that doesn't stop me from wanting her in ways I know I shouldn't.

Although I fail to fucking care that I shouldn't want her. Not when it's clear she wants me as much as I want her.

Not only do I want to fuck her brains out, but I want to care for her too. Something I haven't wanted to do in a long time.

The innocent-looking girl whose emerald eyes have lodged so deep in my mind I seem to see nothing but her. The way she came and the look of innocence on her face when I coated her with my cum in what was the most intense high of my entire life lives in my mind. I didn't even need drugs to achieve it.

Now I'm fucking hooked.

Addicted.

I've swapped one addiction for another. Only, this one is more deadly; she has the ability to render me powerless. Yet I have no intention of heeding the warning bells going off in my mind.

No, I want nothing more than to watch her face as I push my cock into her little pussy. I bet it's so fucking tight too. My cock throbs at imagining slamming inside her so hard she has to cling to me with her small hands. Mmm, I'll mold that little hole so it fits only my cock.

My mind races with thoughts of what she's doing and with whom. Is she sleeping with that kid who had his eyes firmly latched on to her ass?

I should have taken the little prick's eyes out. Sent the little punk home blind for daring to look at what's mine. Because she is mine.

My little girl to protect.

And if anyone tries to take her from me, I'll fucking kill them.

Jade

The door closes with a snick, and I note the light on in the living room. I glance up toward the stairs, tempted to creep up there and go to bed, but something makes me stalk toward the living room, and when I open the door to Tommy sprawled out on the couch, I freeze.

My heart free-falls as I take him in.

He's wearing a white T-shirt and loose joggers that showcase his impressive bulge, which makes me lick my lips at the thought of how he came on my face. I've never seen a cock up close before, and watching him unravel in front of me was the most erotic thing I have ever seen.

His eyes are closed, so I step closer. The dark locks of his tousled hair cover his forehead, and I long to push it back to fully see his face.

He's absolutely gorgeous and totally forbidden. So why do I feel this need to crawl into his lap while his muscled arms flex tightly around me? Why do I crave him so much?

I shake my head and move to step back, but his hand snaps out and grabs me, making me jolt at the roughness behind his touch.

His eyes snap open, glaring daggers at me. "Where the fuck have you been?"

I swallow nervously. "With friends."

He sits up but doesn't release my arm. "What fucking friends? Who? With that guy from the pool?" His eyes narrow on me as my mind struggles to think of what to say.

"Are you fucking him?" His jaw tightens, and his gaze shoots daggers at me.

Is he jealous? Hope flares inside me as heat travels into my cheeks. A little embarrassed at the thought, when my mouth opens, no words come out. I'm rendered dumbstruck at his accusation.

Finally, I take a deep breath and exhale. He parades women through the mansion like they're trophies. How dare he question what I get up to and with whom?

He shakes my arm with anger when I don't answer him. The force behind his touch makes me whimper. "Answer the fucking question!" His temple pulsates, and the veins on his neck protrude.

"No."

"No, what?"

He grabs me by my hips and places me on his lap. *Oh god, I can feel his bulge.* The heat in my face travels over my neck and down my chest.

"No, what?" he snaps again, making me swallow.

"No, I'm not sleeping with him."

His tense body appears to relax as he rests his body back against the pillow with me straddling his thick thighs.

The pads of his thumbs work over my hips in a soothing motion as he watches my face. "Have you ever fucked him?" he asks. His voice is low, with an edge of jealousy in it.

"No," I breathe out with all honesty.

He seems to melt against the back of the couch, pleased with my answer, and all the tension drains from his face. "Good girl." I practically purr at his words, and his lips tip up into a rare, soft smile.

His tongue darts out, trailing over his lower lip, and like a predator, his gaze roams over my body before stopping on the lace of my thin camisole top.

Shuffling slightly, he positions his cock against my center, eliciting a moan.

"Are you going to let Daddy see your tits?" He raises an eyebrow.

My throat is dry, and my heart races with need.

"Let me see, little girl," he coos in a velvety voice while he continues to caress my hips as if coaxing my decision from me.

He glides his thick hand up my arm, and the contact of our skin brushing against one another makes me break out in a shiver that causes my nipples to pebble.

His chest heaves as his eyes flick from mine to my tits and back again. Then, he lowers a strap of my top before repeating the action with the other strap. He shuffles my top below my bra.

Watching his eyes turn heavy and full of want makes me rock against his cock, and he releases a low growl, giving me the confidence to unclip my bra and allow my tits to spill out for him.

He hisses between his teeth and bucks against me. "Fuck, you're beautiful." His words fill me with warmth, making me feel needed, treasured, and protected all in one.

With one hand on my hip and the other stroking over my arm, he encourages me to rock against him. "Good girl. Take what you need from Daddy's cock."

"Oh god." I moan.

The way his filthy mouth works sends a rush of wetness to my panties that I swear will be visible through my shorts too.

"Fuck, little girl. Can Daddy touch your tits?" He licks his lips again and swallows hard, mesmerizing me.

The way he asks me is so forbidden and so full of want my clit throbs against his stiff cock, so I press down and rock harder, grinding against him.

"Yes, please," I beg as I press into his length, causing him to grunt and his eyes to become hooded.

His hand moves quickly, and he bucks up against me as soon as his fingers come into contact with the soft flesh of my tit, as though he's unable to control himself.

"Fuck yes." He groans when his fingers graze over my nipple. "Fuck, Daddy wants to suck these little nipples so bad."

"Ohhh," I moan as I begin to work my hips faster and faster over his solid length. My hands find his shoulders, and I use my nails to anchor myself. He pinches my nipple, sending lightning bolts of desire down my spine and into my panties. Then his mouth swoops in and he tugs my nipple into his mouth while using his teeth to graze the peak, and my eyes roll in pleasure. "Oh god, Daddy. Oh god." I cling to him as my needy body rocks of its own accord.

I grind down on him harder. His tongue lashes over my pebbled peak, and he suckles my nipple into his mouth hungrily. The lapping noise of his greedy mouth against my bare flesh fills the room.

He pulls back, releasing my nipple with a pop to stare at me in awe. His breath is ragged, and his forehead is coated in a sheen of sweat. "Fuck, you're incredible. Rub that pussy on my cock, little girl." His breathing quickens as he thrusts his hips up. "Rub your tight little pussy over my cock. Faster." The hand on my hip moves me faster and faster over his cock. "Make Daddy come, little girl. Make him fucking come."

A loud, unrecognizable noise leaves me when he smacks my tit, then pinches my nipple, sending a flurry of pleasure through me. My tits shake and sway as he fucks up into me. My orgasm erupts. "That's it, give it to Daddy," he encourages.

My body curls tight, and I throw my head back. "Daddy, please."

"Fuck, yes!" His body stills. The hand on my hip and the tight squeeze on my tit grip me firmer as his cock pulsates below me.

Then, as I slowly come down from my orgasm and my rapid breaths regulate, I lift my head to face him. My stomach plummets at the anger coating his features, and heat blossoms deeper over my face. His jaw tics, his body coils tight, and his veins protrude on his forehead.

"Go to bed, little girl," he snipes out. Emotion clogs my throat at his harsh tone.

Hurt lances through my chest at how quickly he's dismissing me. After gifting myself to him that way, he's treating me like just another one of his many whores.

I scramble from his lap and head toward the door, noticing the large wet patch on his joggers from where he came as I rush away.

"Jade."

I freeze and look over my shoulder toward him.

"Lock your door." The danger behind his insinuation is evident. He wants me, but he's angry at me and with himself for wanting it.

As I walk through the door and up the stairs, I do so

with the knowledge I want nothing more than for Daddy to creep into my room at night and take me.

To make me his.

Chapter Seven

Jade

I tiptoe down the stairs, clutching my purse as I head toward the front door, hoping to leave without him knowing. Not that he would care anyway. Why should he? Nobody else ever has.

Tommy has been distant. All I know is it's been almost a week since our last encounter and since then, he's locked himself in his bedroom and I haven't seen him at all.

No doubt he's been drinking himself into oblivion again, and, as usual, at some point during the day, he'll drag himself out of bed late with a hangover and make himself scarce in the huge mansion. Avoiding me, much like he did after the pool party when he shut it down and sent everyone home, then distanced himself from me.

I let jealousy creep in when I wonder if he's fulfilling his needs with the women he pays. Do they call him Daddy, too? The thought has a pool of dread sitting like a rock in my stomach, threatening to expel the meager contents.

Do I mean so little to him? Am I just a toy for him to play with?

I've been at his mansion for almost a fortnight and have yet to see Tommy go to work. My mind wanders over whether he does work. I know his family is part of the Mafia. But I don't know what, if anything, Tommy does for them.

His father must provide for him because there's no way a man can afford the mansion, cars, and lifestyle he has without financial help from somewhere. Not to mention the women he pays.

I can't help but wonder why he doesn't have a girlfriend or why he's not married again. According to the Mafia way of life, by now, he should be married with children of his own. My heart plummets at the thought.

Plus, the man is gorgeous and clearly very wealthy. All his brothers are in relationships. I know this because I've met them at family functions where Tommy was always absent, as though detaching himself from them all.

My hand reaches for the door handle, but it's yanked to the side, forcing me to loosen my grip. Our eyes clash, mine filled with shock and his with rage.

"Where do you think you're going?" His gruff, possessive tone sends a ripple of arousal through me. As if sensing it, his lip turns up into a knowing smirk. *God, I want to slap it away and kiss it better.*

I shake my head, trying to come to my senses. Raising my head and jutting my chin out, I say, "Out."

His eyebrows furrow as he scans over me. There's nothing to see. I'm in leggings and a baggy hoodie, comfy clothes.

"Where?"

Irritation burns my skin. He's been absent all week and now he cares?

I've never had to answer to someone before because nobody has ever cared. Why should I have to answer to someone now? "If you must know, the store."

His gaze drills into me, telling me the questioning isn't going to stop. "What store?"

My shoulders fall lax. "The drugstore."

His spine bolts straight and his eyes widen, the darkness in them consumes his pupils and a flutter of trepidation swims in my stomach at his odd reaction. "For what? Are you sick?" The concern in his voice has a lump forming in my throat, and when he places the palm of his hand on my forehead, I practically melt into him like a pathetic little girl needing reassurance. Tears burn my eyes at the thought, so I shake off his hand, refusing to be that person. To be dependent on someone.

"I'm not sick," I snap and avert my gaze.

But I can feel his eyes on me, and when I look out of the corner of my eye, Tommy studies me for a moment, slowly dragging a finger over his lip as though searching for something. He lowers his tone as if purposely trying an alternative tactic. "Tell me what's wrong, little girl."

A whimper escapes my lips, and my cheeks pinken as I clamp my mouth shut in embarrassment at my reaction.

"Jade?" His once again stern voice cuts through my dazed state.

I breathe out a heavy sigh and face him. "I'm on my period if you must know, and I need supplies. I've run out." I dart my eyes away in embarrassment as heat travels over me, and my hot face flushes bright red.

"On your period?" His gaze roams leisurely over my body, making me fidget under his scrutiny, and when he licks those damn lips like a hungry animal, my body reacts wantonly and my panties become damp with arousal.

He clears his throat. "Come on, little girl. Let's take you to the drugstore."

He lifts his keys from his pocket and opens the front door, and somehow, I follow him to his blacked-out SUV, wanting to die of embarrassment and ride him all at once.

Jesus.

I'll just blame my hormones for how much I want to fuck my stepfather.

Tommy

She wanders up the aisle toward the women's products, and I follow behind like a well-trained dog. Never in my life have I gone shopping with a female. Not even with Justine. And periods are something I avoid. No way do I want to get dragged into that walking nightmare.

Yet, with her, I feel protective. Maybe it's guilt for not being around? Or the fact she has no one else.

Without thinking, I scoff out loud, and heads turn in my direction. I'm lying to myself and fucking know it. Because every part of me wants Jade and not in a father-daughter way.

Seeing her flush bright red had me wondering how far it goes down when she comes. Does it travel as far as her pussy?

I itch to touch her further; I spent the entire week imagining it.

My cock is raw from how hard I've fucked my fist multiple times a day. But nothing comes close to the feel of her skin against mine and the look of innocence on her face while I corrupt her.

When she stops at the tampons, anger surges through me. Does she use those? Does she put them inside her little pussy? She lifts a box from the shelf, and I snatch it from her hand, knocking it to the floor.

Her stunned gaze meets mine.

"Do you use those?" My voice is dark, and she shudders, making me preen with delight. "Do you shove them in your pussy, little girl?" *Jesus, I just can't seem to help myself around her.*

Her mouth opens and closes. Then she swallows audibly, making my cock jump in satisfaction.

"Do you have one shoved in your cunt now?" I raise an eyebrow.

She slowly shakes her head, but it does nothing to temper my anger. "Answer me, little girl," I grit out, as I'm pissed she could be putting things inside her pussy. But more pissed I'm not there to witness it. Fuck, I bet she's tight. Not like the whores I'm used to.

Her voice is a delicate whisper. "I don't."

My shoulders relax. "Good girl. Now, get what you need and let's go. I need to take care of you."

Her eyes flutter closed for a moment, and without thinking, I move forward and bring my lips to hers. I place a soft peck on her lips and relish the moan that escapes from her mouth as her body sinks against mine.

"Good girl," I whisper against her ear, enjoying the shiver that takes over her body at my words and proximity. "Such a good girl for Daddy," I coo while stroking tenderly over her hair.

A soft mewl leaves her, and I feel the noise all the way down to my balls. Will she sound like that when I slide inside her too?

I take a step back, gifting her space to make the right

decision while blocking her view of the forbidden tampons. She picks up a pack of sanitary pads, and I smile at her in approval while she lowers her head and shakes it mockingly.

"You're insane, Tommy." She blows out a breath as she turns and walks toward the counter. I catch up with her in a few strides, take the pads from her, and gift her ass with a tight squeeze.

"That's Daddy to you, little girl." I wink at her as I push past and make my way to pay.

I'm prepared to do whatever it takes to look after what is becoming abundantly clear. Mine. My little girl.

Chapter Eight

Tommy

As soon as we return home, I send Jade upstairs for a bath while I make her a smoothie and fill a plate with sweet treats.

Never in my life have I dealt with a woman during her menstruation. So I do some googling to discover what they need. I'm hoping the drink filled with vitamins and other ingredients, along with the treats women crave, is enough to pacify her.

While taking each step, my cock rubs against my pants, making me groan. Fuck, I need to come on her again. It's the only thing that placates me, if only for a short while.

I seem to have swapped out one addiction for another. Only this one is far sweeter. Far more forbidden and definitely far more rewarding.

Pushing open her bedroom door, her scent wraps around me and makes my body relax—something I only seem to have the ability to do when around her.

Her head pokes up from beneath the frilly pink covers, making me grin at the ridiculousness of them. "You look like a little girl all tucked up in your pretty sheets."

Her eyes sharpen and her lip curls. "Very funny."

I place the tray down on the nightstand and revel at the surprise on her face. "Do you need anything else?"

She shakes her head. "No. Thank you."

"Do you need pain relief?" I raise my eyebrow as I stand over her.

"No. It only hurts a little."

I give her a nod, and she takes a drink of the smoothie while I walk around the opposite side of the bed. She turns her head over her shoulder, and her mouth falls open when I tug my T-shirt over my head, revealing my solid abs. After placing the drink back on the dresser, she turns to face me, and the feel of her gaze on me has electricity shooting through my veins and my cock thickening.

I'm confident in my body. I might be an addict, but I keep myself toned, and tattoos cover my torso down to the sculpted *V*. Her eyes widen further, making me chuckle as I lower my jeans while standing before her in only my boxers with the tip of my cock peeking out the top of my waistband.

She swallows and darts her eyes away, her cheeks flushed with embarrassment.

"T-Tommy, wh-what are you doing?" She grips the comforter in a ball, and her knuckles whiten as she tugs it toward her chest, as though nervous and wanting to cover herself.

I smile at her, unperturbed, climb onto the bed, and pull the comforter from her enough to allow me access to slide beneath.

"I'm going to look after you," I tell her truthfully. The thought of taking care of her makes my body swell with pride and my cock leak with joy.

Before now, any form of responsibility wasn't even an option for me. I point-blank denied it.

She refuses to look at me, making me choke on a laugh at her innocence as I rest my head against the pillow. "Switch the light off and go to sleep, Jade." My husky voice makes her shiver, but I don't have to ask her twice. She quickly leans over the nightstand and fumbles with the switch as she turns the light off before rolling onto her side and facing away from me.

The light from beneath the bathroom door illuminates the room, allowing me to see her. With a heavy sigh, I roll onto my side to face her and tug her sharply against me, my chest to her back. I grind my hard cock against her perky little ass, making her freeze.

"Tommy?" she whispers.

Anger at the use of my name prickles my skin. How she can so easily flit between Daddy and Tommy, whereas I'm stuck with Daddy playing over and over in my head, making me in-fucking-sane with need for her.

I wind an arm beneath the pillow, trailing it up toward her throat, where I grip it. "Stop with the Tommy. You know how much you like calling me Daddy, and you know how much I like to hear it." Her chest rises and falls rapidly, and her skin heats beneath my hand as her pulse races.

"Okay, Daddy."

A groan catches in my throat, and I push against her, gifting her with a kiss on her bare shoulder. "Such a good girl." She whimpers at my term of endearment. One we're both becoming accustomed to.

Removing my hand from her throat, I trail it down the side of her slim body and past the swell of her tits toward her stomach, where I use my palm to circle it in a smoothing motion.

I repeat the process I researched, gently circling her stomach with the flat of my hand, soothing her.

"Does this help?" I ask in a delicate whisper against her hair.

"Y-yes."

She settles against me while I continue to massage her, hoping to take away any pain.

"Mmm." I continue the motion on her stomach, and slowly, she allows herself to relax against me. My cock sits in the crook of her ass cheeks, with only the thin fabric of her little sleep shorts and panties keeping us apart.

I lower my hand and she stills. "Let Daddy take care of you."

Her whole body has become tense. "Shhh," I soothe.

My fingers slip beneath the waistband of her shorts and into her panties. "Relax, little girl. Let Daddy play with your pussy."

"I . . ." The panic in her voice has me grinning like an ass. "I'm bleeding."

"Mmm, I know." A deep, primal groan leaves me as I push against her, rubbing my cock into her ass again and again.

"Oh god." She moans as my fingers travel past the edge of her sanitary pad. "Let me play in your blood, little girl." I lick her neck, and she moans in response. My cock throbs in joy, and precum leaks from the tip as I gather her wetness and refuse to push my finger into her hole as much as I want to.

No, my cock will be the one to do that.

"Daddy," she pants as I apply a little pressure to her swollen clit. Her breathing becomes irregular, and my balls tighten with how turned on I am now.

"Fuck," I groan in pleasure at the warmth of her essence on my fingertips and the thrust of her ass tormenting my cock.

If I don't do something soon, I'll be coming in my boxers. Not a fucking chance when I have my girl in bed with me.

"Daddy's getting his cock out," I whisper against her ear, making her gasp as I push down my boxers, and my cock springs free, all while I keep the circular rhythm going with my fingers.

I push my cock against her ass, and the stickiness of my precum coats her. My eyes roll. "Fuck, that feels good, little girl. Your bare skin against my cock." An urge to slam into her is almost overwhelming, but I want to look after her tonight—like I should have been doing.

"I want to feel you against me, Daddy," she pants, almost whiny, causing precum to drip at her words.

"Fuck," I grunt out. I tug her sleep shorts and panties down to her thighs, earning a grumble of shock from her.

"I'm bleeding," she shrieks.

"I know, but it's okay. Daddy doesn't mind." I place a reassuring kiss against her shoulder, and she melts against me, allowing me to play in her blood. Fuck, it feels incredible.

Slowly, I apply a little pressure to her shoulder, encouraging her to roll more onto her side, therefore allowing her perfect little ass to stick higher in the air.

"Mmm. Fuck, your ass is incredible. Daddy wants to

fuck it so bad." I grip her ass cheek, making her jump, and chuckle at how nervous and innocent she is. Such a fucking turn-on. "It's okay. I only want to play." Using the head of my cock, I swipe it up and down the crack of her ass. My balls draw up each time the head contacts her puckered hole. "Fuck, that's good, little girl. Daddy loves playing with your little asshole."

I press harder on her clit, and she arches against my cock, probably without meaning to. A growl rumbles inside me as I watch in awe as my cock leaks over her asshole. A fierce need to push past her forbidden barrier and fill her with my cum radiates from me. Every muscle in my body is pulled tight to stop myself.

"Daddy wants to play in your ass, little girl."

I bite into her shoulder, making her wince, but she pushes back when I slap a hand down sharply on her pussy. "Oh god."

"Daddy wants to put the tip of his cock inside your little hole." I fist my cock as I slide it up and down, applying a little pressure around her asshole on each downstroke. My breathing becomes more erratic with each contact. More desperate. I want nothing more than to drive into her. Make her scream as my cock tears through her ass. But I want to protect her more, make her feel good.

"Are you going to let Daddy come inside it?" I kiss her again.

"Oh god." She whimpers and pushes back against me.

I rest the tip against her hole, my precum gifting it with the perfect amount of lubrication. "Push back on Daddy's cock and let him put the tip inside. Let him spill his cum inside you. Just a little." I beg, trying to refrain from sinking inside her without consent.

My fist works faster and faster, and the slapping sound

of our flesh fills the air. "Tell me," I grind out on a growl. "Tell me I can spill my cum inside you," I grunt. "Say, 'Daddy, you can put the tip in.' Tell Daddy you want your tiny hole stretching for him."

"Oh god, Daddy." I slap her pussy again as I struggle to rein in my impending orgasm.

"Daddy needs to come, little girl. Tell me what you need . . ."

She moans loudly when I press down on her clit, rubbing furiously. "Please, please put the tip in. Please stretch my hole and come inside my ass."

"Thank fuck." I take the creamy flesh of skin on her shoulder between my teeth and tug as I push the head of my cock against her asshole. Her skin stretches around me, and I sink my teeth into her flesh harder to try and stop myself from coming before I breach her barrier.

"Ahhhh!" she screams as her orgasm hits her, and three of my fingers rub her faster and faster. Blood coating each of them. "Daddy!" She pushes back against my cock, allowing me to fist myself as the tip of my cock swells inside her stretched asshole. The sight of me breaching her hole and stretching it tight is my undoing.

"Oh fuck. Fuck, little girl." My cock pulsates, and the veins swell as the engorged tip expands to allow my cum to spurt from me in an explosion of exhilarating pleasure. "Holy fuckkkk."

I hold her in place as our breathing regulates.

"Mmm, I could sleep inside you like this, Jade." I kiss the bite mark, and she winces, making me smile against her torn skin. Then, as our bodies become spent, I place tender kisses on the surrounding area.

She glances over her shoulder. "I'm bleeding, don't

forget." She nods down toward her waist, making me chuckle at how much bleeding on me unnerves her.

"I know." I grin back at her, desperate to lower my fingers into her bloody hole and show her how much I really don't care about the mess we've created.

Instead, I give her the comfort I know she craves. With a heavy sigh, I slide my cock from her ass, and a sense of pride fills me when my cum spills from it. "Fuck, you look hot with my cum dripping out of you." She stills, her whole body hardens, making annoyance rumble inside me. I tug her panties and shorts up and roll her onto her back so I can see her pretty face and those sparkling green eyes.

"What's wrong?" I ask, scanning over her face. The way she froze, as though suddenly panicked, has me desperate to fix whatever is wrong.

She licks her lips with apprehension in her eyes, then darts them away. I reluctantly tuck my cock back into my boxers and then turn her chin to face me—blood now marks her chin. The sight is fucking beautiful.

Her breath brushes over the tips of my fingers, sending a wave of need through me. But first, I need to know why she froze on me.

"Jade," I admonish harshly.

She bites into her lip as though unsure of speaking her mind. My fingers grip her tighter, letting her know there's no escaping me.

She rolls her eyes before bringing them back to mine. "How many women have you done that with?" She swallows slowly. "Do I need to get checked?"

Fire fills my body and rage makes my blood pump faster, but when I see the unshed tears in her eyes mixed with vulnerability, my anger dissipates. I have a sudden need to reassure her. With my eyes fixed on hers, I tell her truthfully, "I've never had unprotected sex, Jade."

Her lips fall open and her pupils widen in disbelief. "Never?"

"No." I release her and drop my head back against my pillow, tugging her against me to lie on my chest. "Not even in the only relationship I've ever had," I admit lowly.

She lifts her head and rests her palms on my chest, placing her head on them to stare back at me. It's not lost on me how clean and innocent her skin is next to my tattooed olive skin. Clean against dirty. The fingerprints of blood on her chin show me how tarnished she's becoming under my touch. I should leave her alone, not stain her further. Leave her as perfect as she is now. Yet I can't. I won't. I fucking crave her.

"Why did you break up?"

Sighing heavily, I stare back at her, unsure of whether to allow not only her but me, too, to delve into my past. I'd be discussing it for the first time in years with the only other girl I've ever felt something for.

"She left," I say simply.

"Why?"

"I don't know." I huff out, answering honestly. Because although there's so much more to the story, that's the part that hurts the most. The part that won't allow me to move on.

My heart is beating faster, and I know she can feel it too, but she doesn't acknowledge it. Instead, she draws lazy circles over my chest, tracing the tattoos covering my skin, and it soothes me. It gives me the reassurance I crave to give her.

"My family didn't want us to be together," I admit as

the anger simmers, unlike the way it normally boils beneath my skin. She grounds me.

"Is that why you don't like spending time with them? Because you blame them?"

This time, I can't hide the venom I feel. "They took her away from me. I just don't know how to prove it," I bite out with certainty. "They refuse to tell me where she is." I exhale loudly and stare up at the ceiling as I struggle with the conversation. "I tried. I tried to be what my father wanted me to be. I thought if I married your mother, then he'd be satisfied and give me what I want. But he always wanted more."

Her finger doesn't stop moving, nor do my lips. "He wanted me to fulfill my duty as a Mafia son and have an heir with her." I scoff at the notion. "Little did he realize your mother was just as fucked up as me."

Her finger stops, severing the connection and making my head dart up off the pillow to check on her. Hurt coats her features, and I want to kick myself for being the one to put it there.

I graze my fingers down her cheek. "I'm sorry."

She swallows hard. "It's okay. She was fucked up." She glances away to cover the emotion painted on her face, and I feel like a fucking ass.

Then she rests her head against my chest, making me feel whole once again, and this time, I find it's me soothing her. My hand strokes gently over her hair in appreciation. Jesus, I could lie like this forever.

"She didn't want me. So I'm pleased you didn't bring another child into the world, Tommy." There's a long, silent pause. "When I have a baby, it'll be mine and my husband's everything. We're going to be the perfect family. Like every child deserves."

Pain hits me square in the chest, and I fidget as I try to disguise that I'm struggling to breathe. The thought of her being with anyone else but me hurts, and the fact she's discussing having a family with them feels like a knife has been plunged into my heart. She's mine to protect.

Her soft breathing tells me she's slipping into a slumber.

"You belong to me, little girl," I whisper, meaning every word. "I'll kill anyone that tries to take you from me. You belong to me."

Chapter Nine

Tommy

I slept incredibly last night with Jade tucked safely in my arms. And instead of being haunted by nightmares of Justine leaving me, I dreamed of Jade's eyes. Her green orbs were so bright they forced the darkness to slip away, and when she smiled, warmth spread through my entire body. Finally, I feel alive. She makes me want more, and most importantly, she makes me want to be more too, her softness a contrast to my rigid, heartless form. Her feistiness and fire a challenge I live for, and her sexy innocence a desire I crave.

I've never wanted to protect and fuck someone as much as I do her, and with that realization, I gather the bottles from around my house like a crackhead in a drug factory before tossing them all in the trash.

If I want Jade in my life, then I need to be a good role model.

I need to be a good daddy.

After knocking on her bedroom door and finding her room vacant, I search the movie room and pool area before finally taking out my phone. My heart races at her absence. How am I meant to protect her when I don't even know where she is? How can I care for her properly when she's not with me?

My fingers tighten on my phone. "Marshall. Where is she?" I bark out.

"Sir?" he questions, making me want to reach into the phone and wring his useless neck.

"Jade? Where the fuck is my daughter?" My heart thuds as panic fills my bloodstream. Has she left me? Is she out with one of those guys from the pool? Is she fucking one of them? All of them? After what we did last night, did it mean nothing to her?

"She's at work, sir."

My body jolts in shock at his words. "Work?" I question in confusion. My mind races with the conversation I had with my father. I'm fucking sure he never mentioned my daughter worked.

"Yes, sir. Miss Jade works at a local bakery store."

"Work?" No women in our family ever worked. Us Mafia men look after our women. Support them, providing everything they need. Anger burns under my skin, fighting to break loose. Who the fuck authorized this? My father?

Well, she's mine to look after now.

Mine to protect.

"Give me all the details. Now!" I bark down the phone before slamming it on the kitchen counter as I try to regulate my breathing.

Gripping the counter with my hands, I close my eyes and drop my head. Don't worry, little girl. Daddy will look after you from now on.

Jade

I lift the muffins from the tray, blowing on my fingers from the heat of them, then arrange them on the cooling rack.

When I left for work this morning, I was relieved to find Tommy had left my bed. The evidence of the night before coated the sheets, and embarrassment washed over me. I never knew you could experience such pleasure while on your period, no less. My ass is a little tender, but I can't deny it was hot as hell, and even though I hate the thought of him being with other women, that he has only ever not used protection with me feels like a gift. It makes me feel treasured and important to him. Like he's given a part of himself to me he hasn't given to anyone else.

Melinda, my boss, pokes her head into the kitchen area. "Jade, there's a guy here for you." She motions with her head toward the shop front. My eyebrows furrow. None of the guys from school ever come in here. Maybe Darryl decided to pay me a visit.

"He says he's your daddy?"

I choke on thin air. The saliva in my throat feels trapped because, surely, she's not referring to Tommy, right?

She glances back over her shoulder before looking back at me again, her eyes alight with the flirtation I've become accustomed to. My shoulders stiffen and my grip on the tray tightens with jealousy.

"He's hot," She tacks on, grating on my nerves. I slam the tray onto the counter with a huff and push past her as I head into the front of the store.

There, roaming around the store with his hands on his hips is the man that came in my ass yesterday. The one that haunts my dreams with promises of punishment and pleasure. His broad shoulders pull his shirt firmly across his back, and I whimper when he lifts a cupcake from the shelf as his rolled-up sleeves expose his tattooed forearms. I run my gaze over the veins that protrude from his arms, making me want to lick them. Oh god, what has he done to me?

His tongue darts out and flicks over the frosting, sending a wave of wetness into my panties before he plucks the cherry off the top and then he lifts his eyes to meet mine. My body stills as our eyes remain locked on one another.

Desire fills the air, and when he pops the cherry between his teeth, heat travels up my neck, and I can feel the flush of my cheeks at the silent insinuation behind the action. He winks at me, making me gasp in shock.

Surely he doesn't know.

My pulse races and my legs quiver. *Holy shit.*

"I didn't know you had a job, Jade." He grins at me as he bites into the cupcake again, with his teeth bared to me like a wild animal, and the predatory look in his eyes tells me I'm his prey and he's about to eat me alive.

I'm frozen to the spot as he pushes the rest of the cake into his mouth before making a languorous show of slipping his fingers past his lips and sucking off the frosting that was barely there to begin with. All the while, my heart is in my throat as I watch on, transfixed by the sheer sexual chemistry rolling off him.

The pop of his fingers exiting his mouth—a mere replica of the sound of his thumb leaving my lips not so long ago—sends a wave of need coursing through me.

A sly, knowing smirk plays out on his handsome face, and annoyance rumbles inside me for allowing my reaction to him to happen.

I clear my throat. "You're not interested in me. Why would you know where I work?" I snap back as I rub my hands on my apron, trying my best to diminish my feelings.

His grin falls from his face as he steps forward, all seriousness now taking over his once playful features. "Oh, but I am interested in you, Jade. You're my little girl to protect." He tucks a lock of hair behind my ear and the sweet gesture has my body swaying toward him. "I had the tip of my cock in your ass last night and the blood of your period coating my fingers, little girl. You belong to me now. You're mine."

My blood races wildly through me, and my body heats at the crudeness of his words. Yet I want more. Need more. Need him, my daddy.

Moving closer, he places his hands on either side of my face. "Be a good girl and go grab your things." He flicks his eyes toward the back of the store.

I swallow. "I . . . I haven't finished my shift yet."

Tommy sighs heavily and places a gentle kiss on my forehead. "Yes, you have. Off you go now. Do as Daddy tells you." His eyes drill into mine. The darkness in them seems oddly brighter somehow. I nod as though in a trance, desperate to please him.

Untying my apron, I turn toward the kitchen, unsure of what is happening. All I know is Tommy Marino might be my stepfather, but I want him to be my daddy.

Chapter Ten

Jade

I sit with my hands in my lap and stare down at my thighs as Tommy glares straight ahead at the road. I don't miss the feeling of his eyes on me every few seconds. Nor the way his gaze lingers on the apex of my tight T-shirt that showcases my tits.

Eventually, he clears his throat. "Do you want to tell me why you work there?"

Finally lifting my head, I cast my gaze over toward his. "I need the money."

He scoffs, and my temper skyrockets. "For what?"

"For things, Tommy. Not all of us have a family to sponge off of." I slap a hand over my mouth, realizing that I said the words aloud. He jolts, then swallows thickly. His features and shoulders fall as though disappointed at my comment, but screw him. *He will not make me feel bad for taking care of myself. He can't even take care of himself.*

"You're right."

His normally angry eyes meet mine with a softness I've

never seen. "I'm sorry." He glances away. "But you shouldn't have to provide for yourself. Not when my family can provide for you."

I open my mouth to tell him I can look after myself, that I always have. But when his eyes lock with mine and he speaks, I'm stunned to silence. "I want to provide for you, Jade. You're mine to protect, mine to care for. You're simply mine. My little girl."

My heart skips a beat, and my eyes fill with tears. I've never once felt wanted in my entire life. Now, a man I barely know claims to want me, and in this moment, I don't care if it's temporary or because of some crazy taboo attraction we have going with one another because there's nothing I want more than to be his. To be protected by him.

He takes my hand from my lap, gently kissing my fingers before placing my hand over his heart.

"Feel that?" The rhythm of his heart seems to beat in time with mine. My glazed eyes latch on to his, and I give him a small nod. "It's finally beating again." He licks his lips and swallows past a lump in his throat. "For you," he adds, making my heart soar with emotion.

His words send a shiver down my spine, and I part my lips to ask more, but the shrill sound of his phone fills the car.

He sighs heavily and drops my hand before putting the call on loudspeaker; I immediately miss the contact of his warmth.

"Rocco," he drones, as though annoyed—referring to his younger brother. Tommy quickly takes my hand from my lap with a frown and places it on his thigh. Happiness spreads through me at the simple gesture, and the fact I can feel the heat of his skin seeping through the fabric makes me squeeze his thigh tighter, earning a smile from him that warms me deep inside.

"I need a favor." Rocco's deep voice is hushed.

Tommy grinds his teeth. It's obvious he's pissed because he doesn't usually get involved in the family business. "What this time?" he snaps, and I realize he clearly isn't as detached from the family as he allows everyone to believe.

"There's been some trouble at Base. Can you swing by and sort it out?" You can hear the hope in Rocco's voice.

Tommy's jaw tightens, and he pinches the bridge of his nose, clearly reluctant to help his younger brother.

"Dude, please?" The sound in Rocco's voice is desperate, but Tommy doesn't acknowledge it. Instead, he exhales loudly in contempt.

"Fine," he snipes out.

"Thanks, brother," Rocco replies with confidence, and the words are filled with gratitude.

Tommy grunts in response and ends the call.

"Sorry, little girl. Detour."

He spins the car around, making me shriek as his laughter fills the car. A sound I'll never tire of hearing.

Tommy

"Stay by my side, okay?" My eyes drill into her panicked ones as she takes in the imposing building. My lip quirks up at the side at how innocent and vulnerable she appears beside me, all feistiness gone. "Daddy will look after you," I whisper as I press my lips against hers. She opens her mouth to accept me, but I pull back with a smile, relishing how hungry she is for me. I wonder if she'll be as desperate when I fuck her tight little ass or finally slip into her pussy?

I adjust my cock blatantly as I climb out of the SUV and round the car to open the door for her. Her startled green eyes make my chest swell with pride as she places her small hand in mine and slides out of the SUV and against my body, embracing my protection. Glancing down at our entwined hands, my blood warms with possession at how my large hand engulfs her small one. *Fuck, that feels good.*

The sound of the bass fills the air as I scan my free hand over the screen, allowing us access to one of my family's many nightclubs.

Pulling her through the metal door, I nod at my security as we force our way through the crowds of people on the dance floor. The scent of drugs fills my nostrils, and my body craves to partake in the euphoria like the addict I am. But not when I have my own little addiction so close, not when I need to protect her above all else.

Naked women slide down the poles with their bare pussies and tits on display while men scream lewd remarks at them and beg the women to perform acts on one another.

Jade stiffens beside me, but I pull her along, ignoring her tense posture as we make our way up the metal staircase toward my brother's office.

I scan my hand over the security panel again and tug her into the room. Spinning to face her, my heart races in panic at how her sparkling green eyes appear terrified. I hate how scared she appears when all I want to do is make her feel protected in my care. "I've got you, little girl." I kiss the top of her head and wrap my arms around her, letting her melt into my reassurance.

"Do you normally . . ." She swallows loudly. "Do you normally do all of those things down there?" She blushes while glancing toward the one-way window that showcases the club below.

I pull back to stare into her eyes, and as much as I don't want to disappoint her, I can't lie. She deserves the part of me that wants to become more for her.

"I did," I admit and wait for the look of horror to mar her face. My heart thuds against my chest, expecting her to pull away from me in disgust, but she doesn't.

"I won't anymore." I stare into her emeralds, hoping she can see the truth behind my words. "I don't want to. Not when I have you."

Her face breaks out into the smile I've come to live for. The one I put there.

She gifts me with a coy nod, then moves toward the glass screen and takes in the club.

I hate that she can see everything. All the filth happening just below us and outside the door.

Making my way over to my brother's desk, I turn on the security cameras and press Call on my phone. "Send him up." I end the call.

"Jade. Sit on the couch, please." I point toward the two couches. Even the thought of her innocent skin touching them makes the hairs on my neck prickle with discomfort. She shouldn't be here. Anger builds inside me. What the fuck was I thinking bringing her here?

She doesn't move a muscle, and my jaw tics in frustration as she watches from the glass screen.

"Jade!" I bark, then soften when she jumps at my harsh tone. "Sit on the couch, please." I point over at the couch again.

She moves quickly this time, perching her cute ass on the couch, and my shoulders relax now that she's away from the glass screen, just in time for the buzzer to sound on the door. I flick my eyes up to the security screen and press the door release to allow Z, one of the security guys, to bring in the man who's been causing issues. He throws him into the room, making him stumble through the entrance.

I rest my ass against the side of the desk with my arms crossed over my chest. "What the fuck's the issue?" I ask Z with annoyance in my tone. This shit is eating into time with my girl, not to mention the fact I'm pissed I had to bring her here.

"Fucker caught with his hands in the till." He spits down at the guy's feet. "His name's Trey, he's a barman." My eyes narrow on the little fucker. Sure, I'm pissed this prick tried stealing from us, but this is something Z could have dealt with. The silent conversation we have, with me conveying this information back to him, prompts him to elaborate further. "He's fucked up one of the dancers. She won't step foot in the club again." He spits at the piece of shit again. My blood pumps erratically through my body. If there's one thing our family and business won't stand for, it's the ill-treatment of women and children. "She's in the hospital, Tommy." He drags a hand through his hair. "Broken bones and cut-up face. Poor girl is a fucking mess."

Trey's eyes slice toward Jade, and just like that, all my restraint is lost. How dare he look at what's mine!

"Motherfucker!" I grab him by his throat, dragging him to his full height before spinning him around to slam his face into the desk. The loud crack is evidence of the strength behind my force. "You don't look at her again, fucker." I slam his face again and again as his arms flay beside him. Blood splatters over the woodwork as he screams in agony. I'm relentless in my treatment of him as my mind whirls with thoughts of him hurting my girl too.

Like background noise, Jade cries out, but I pay no attention, not when a monster like this needs extinguishing from the world.

Finally, I release him, allowing him to fall to the ground, a bloody, crumpled mess. "You're fucking lucky my girl is here with me tonight. Otherwise, I'd take your fucking eyes out," I spit, not missing Z's quick glance in Jade's direction.

I tug the handgun from behind my back and aim it at the dumb fuck's head. If he thinks he is leaving this place alive, he's even stupider than we originally thought. I pop the bullet off into his head and revel in his body falling to the floor with a heavy thud.

"Tidy this piece of shit up." I give the heavy deadweight a swift kick.

"Yes, sir." Z grins.

"Jade. Come." I hold my hand out for her, and when her soft hand slips into mine, all tension is drained from me.

She may just be the cure to my addictions.

The door closes behind Z, and all the fury I felt at the sick prick daring to glance at my girl boils to the surface once again. I spring into action, needing her so desperately I swipe the whole contents of the desk onto the floor, and they scatter with a crash.

Jade jumps in shock, making me smile manically while I step toward her. Without warning her, I lift her onto the desk. "Lie back, little girl. Let Daddy have a taste of you." Her eyes bug out, but she complies by lowering herself against the wooden desk while I lower myself to my knees. It's not lost on me that I'm kneeling in the blood of the man I just shot, but the thought makes my cock twitch with a wild need to pleasure her while bathing in his blood. "Lift your dress. Let me see your little panties."

With shaky hands, she lifts the edge of her dress, giving me a full view of her innocent little cotton panties. My steel cock begs for relief, but I ignore it, and instead, I breathe in her pussy and lower my head to give her mound a gentle kiss, flicking my tongue over the fabric. Jesus, she's fucking incredible. My body comes alive above her.

"Oh god, Daddy."

"Mmm, that's it, moan for Daddy, little girl." I suck on her panties, allowing the warmth of my breath to spread over her. She bucks her hips up, spurring me on. "Push your panties to the side. Let me see your bleeding little hole."

Glancing up, I watch in ecstasy as her lips part on my

words before gazing back down in time to see her trembling hands slide her panties to the side. And Jesus, what a sight. Her pussy is pink and wet, glistening with her arousal. I breathe out, struggling to rein in a desperate need to fuck her ruthlessly, brutally even. The wild feeling inside of me is boiling to a pinnacle high, but I want her in my bed when I fuck her for the first time. When I finally push into her hole, I want to devour her and have her screaming at me for mercy while I ravish her little body.

Watching that piece of shit's eyes land on my girl had me crazed to the point of insanity. I wanted to tear his limbs from his body and rip out his insides while he pleaded for mercy. But I didn't want to scare my girl. I want to be her savior, not her monster. As I kneel before her in his blood, I can't help but drag the tips of my fingers through it, relishing in the warmth. Knowing I protected her, saved her. Became her daddy.

Jade watches me closely as I lift my fingers to show her his blood and how merciful I can be for her. Her pupils dilate, and I'm unsure if it's fear in her eyes or something else. Something more. I've no time to analyze it, as I'm worried she's going to withdraw from me when she's just now coming around to the idea of us.

Instead, I trail my fingers up her thighs, smearing blood in their wake. Fuck me, she looks incredible. Bloodied and begging for me. Dropping my head, I kiss her legs with a tenderness I don't feel, then give her a languorous lick from the bottom of her pussy hole to the top. I groan when I swipe my tongue down again, curling it into her hole before dragging it all the way back up her slit.

"Oh, Jesus," she pants. Her knuckles whiten as she clings to her dress. "More. Please, more," she begs, pushing her ass up. My cock throbs so hard it drips precum down my leg, soaking through my boxers and, no doubt, my pants, forcing a growl of appreciation to leave me. Fuck me, she's incredible.

I create a *V* with my fingers and separate her small wet folds, allowing me to nuzzle into her little pussy. My tongue thrashes up and down her slit, like a man possessed, the blood on her thighs makes me feral, and when she grinds against my face, her thighs try to close, but the hand gripping her thigh tightens, and she squeaks in pain at my hold. Closing my eyes, I will my fingers to press so deep into her skin that the marks I leave behind remain permanent. I want them embedded in her like she's embedded in me.

My tongue works down toward her ass, and I smile when I feel her tense. "Mmm, Daddy wants to lick your innocent ass too, little girl." A groan leaves her as if she's going to fight me. I don't give her a chance. When my tongue swirls around her puckered hole and my fingers circle her clit, her legs quiver, making me preen in delight before paying attention to her needy clit, the bud swollen for attention. I suck it into my mouth. "Daddy, I . . . I'm going to . . ." My eyes roll closed at her words, her whole body coiling tight as she throws her head back while I continue to eat her pussy like a man possessed.

When her body finally floats down from the euphoria of my touch, she lifts her head to watch me. Our gazes lock, my body freezes, and we hold one another hostage—an unspoken conversation takes place when I press my lips tenderly to the blood on her thighs.

Mine.

And I'll kill anyone that tries to look at her.

"Yours," she breathes out as if hearing my thoughts.

Chapter Eleven

Tommy

When I brought her to the restaurant, I wasn't expecting my cock to get hard over her simply eating her meal. She pushes another piece of broccoli into her mouth, and I groan when her lips clamp down. Fuck, how does she make eating vegetables look so damn seductive?

My eyes haven't left hers, trying to get a gauge on her lack of response toward me killing someone today, then tongue fucking her while coating her thighs in his blood. But I find no clue as to how she feels about it, and it unnerves me. Does she see me differently now?

"Did I scare you when I put a bullet in his head?" I ask, staring boldly at her. I study her reaction as she lowers her fork.

Our gazes lock. "No," she replies, and I lift my eyebrow in surprise. "I saw my father kill people before." She shrugs.

I nod in understanding. Her father was a capo for our

don, Lorenzo, and when he was killed, he gifted her mother to me. No doubt, my father had filled his head with stories about how his son refused to marry a good Mafia girl, and when they threatened to cut off all my money along with my balls, I was left with no choice but to marry the widow I'd barely even heard of.

It was more of a business move than anything else. It allowed Zenya to keep her dead husband's money, then was passed over to me.

Little did they know she had addictions far greater than mine. Or maybe they did, and she was the ultimate punishment. Two miserable junkies together, self-destructing and rejecting the Mafia life, hoping along the way for an heir to succeed where they didn't.

Zenya didn't last a year before she was found with a needle in her arm and some ridiculous love note claiming to want to join the love of her life. She never considered the daughter banished to boarding school like an inconvenience, and shamefully, neither did I. I only knew about her existence after Zenya's death when my father informed me she had a daughter. To say I was pissed was an understatement. Not only did I have to marry a widow, but she had already birthed a child and now I was being left in charge of one. Not even my own flesh and blood. I had no intentions of parenting someone else's child, and I walked out of his office telling him so while he shook his head in shame.

Perhaps if they had allowed me to marry Justine, they would have had a herd of children.

I felt gratification at the fact that Zenya had essentially committed suicide. The confines had been broken and I was free. If only my addictions were as easy to break.

I take a swig of my water, refusing to drink in Jade's

presence, not when I know one will not be enough, and I refuse to endanger her with my lack of control. Not when she needs someone to protect her.

Not when she needs me.

Jade

I place my knife and fork together while eyeing Tommy carefully. He's been quiet, as though deep in thought, and I can't help but wonder if he regrets what we've done, nerves swim in my stomach. Never could I have imagined how incredible it would feel for someone to eat my pussy. The blood on my thighs is an indicator of the lengths Tommy is prepared to go to keep me safe. But why do I get this dreaded feeling he's regretting it?

Have I been so naive as to think someone cares for me? Wants me?

"Stop it."

I lift my eyes to meet his. "Whatever thought put that worrying look on your face, stop thinking about it."

His lips tip up into an unusual smile, and I mirror it. The air is thick between us as people move around the restaurant. Conversations take place, but our focus is only on one another and they become white noise.

"Oh, Tommy. Fancy seeing you here." His spine straightens and the veins in his neck pulsate as he turns his head to face the woman now standing beside him.

I take her in, she's in business attire with a pencil skirt and white blouse, and the buttons threaten to burst under the bulge of her tits. She has long blonde hair down to her hips in thick waves, and her lips are painted red to match her long fingernails, now grasping his shoulder like a sign of ownership.

My hands ball into fists beneath the table as I scrunch my napkin at her, touching him like she owns him.

He shrugs off her hand and pushes back in his chair to stand, greeting her with a kiss on each cheek. Her eyes practically swim in desire as she swoons around him. "When should we meet again?" She trails her hand down his chest, making me grind my teeth, willing him to bat her hand away.

His hand moves quickly, taking hold of hers and dropping it before he casts his eyes toward me and then quickly back to her. She doesn't miss the movement though, and her body tightens at his subtle glance toward me.

"Who's this?" she asks, waving her hand in my direction. "Are you going to introduce us?"

"Yes, Tommy. Are you going to introduce us?" I bite out. The snideness in my tone clear.

He side-eyes me, threatening punishment for my tone, but I lift my chin in defiance and he chokes on a sardonic laugh. His lip forms into a smirk, and I wait with bated breath as he opens his mouth. "This is my daughter, Jade." He smiles at her.

Fucking smiles!

My veins fill with fury.

"Oh, yes. I decorated your bedroom for you."

She slaps her hand up against her mouth in a mock gasp. "Oh. I thought you were a little younger. I'm sorry, sweetie. I bet you've almost outgrown it, haven't you?"

Almost?

My eyes narrow on the patronizing bitch.

She continues to flutter her fake lashes at Tommy, who makes no attempt to stop her flirtation.

"Who are you?" I spit, unable to hide my temper.

Tommy smirks but otherwise ignores my show of contempt in her direction. "This is Jenna, my father's secretary."

"Huh. One of your many whores, no doubt." I gift him a serene smile that wipes the lust-filled look from the secretary's face.

Tommy's jaw sharpens. "Jade, enough!" The fact he's trying to tell me off, in front of his whore no less, pisses me off. How he can slip into a father-daughter act of a different kind.

I push back in my chair, making customers turn in my direction. "You know what? I think I need to vomit." I throw my napkin onto the table and ignore them as I make my way toward the restroom.

***

I splash the ice-cold water against my face again, and when my focus lands on the mirror, I jolt when I see Jenna leaning against the restroom wall, staring right back at me with a look of venom on her carefully made-up face.

She sighs mockingly. "Tommy needs a woman that's strong and experienced. Not some silly *little girl* that doesn't know her ass from her clit."

My heart hammers as her words burrow deep in my chest. I am inexperienced, and her use of my nickname makes me feel like she can see right through me, through us.

And she's picking us apart bit by bit. My heart hammers and my veins fill with dread.

"You know how filthy he is, right? How he needs more than one woman to get off. To satisfy his urges." She licks her lips. "A *little girl* like you can't possibly satisfy a man like Tommy Marino." Her cruel eyes gleam sinisterly.

Of course, I didn't know that. I've not even considered it. Why would I?

What I know is that I don't want to share him. I can't be that person for him, no matter how much I want him.

She smiles cunningly. "He likes all dirty things." My heart hammers with how well she knows him. I know this part of him only too well myself. But not like her. Jealousy and hurt make my lip tremble, and I fight back the tears pooling in my eyes.

"He likes to watch women fuck one another," she adds, as though waiting for my reaction.

My chest tightens and my pulse races as I resist the urge to let the tears flow.

"Will you give him that, *little girl?* Mmm, while he licks his addiction from your tits?" I squeeze my eyes closed at her words and turn my face, unable to accept the truth.

Before now, I refused to acknowledge Tommy having addictions, much like my mother's.

"Of course, you'll never have a future together. You are father and daughter, after all. It's sick and others will think so too." She clucks while picking at her long talons. "Such a shame for a girl with so much life to be drained and crushed by the Mafia lifestyle. By a man that lives so far in the past that he can't possibly see a future." My body vibrates with the hurt swimming in my blood, and still, she continues on. "You'll never be anything compared to her, you know that, right? And if she ever does come back, where will that leave you?"

She's right. Where would that leave me?

I'd never try and stand in the way of the love of his life. The one he gave his family up for. Not that I'd stand a chance anyway.

I push past her, ignoring her taunting laugh as I throw open the restroom door and head toward the emergency exit.

I'll have nothing and nobody.

Again.

My chest tightens at the realization, and my vision blurs as I wave down a cab.

I need to stay away from Tommy Marino and his filthy words.

I don't need anyone, not even a daddy.

Chapter Twelve

Tommy

As soon as Jade leaves the table, I push my body against Jenna's. Her eyes light up with desire, but I shut it down just as quickly. My stare burns into hers, making her take a step back in shock. I turn my tone to menacing, something she's not used to. "Don't mess with my family, Jenna. I'm fucking warning you. You know what I'm capable of." My eyes bore into hers. "If you try and hurt her, I'll hunt you down and skin you alive." Judging by the bob of her throat, she understands the implication and grants me a nod as she takes another step back.

She clears her throat. "If you'll excuse me." She walks toward the bar while I lower myself back into the chair and wait for Jade to return.

I check my watch before glancing over my shoulder toward the restroom, and anxiety ripples through me. And finally, after fifteen fucking minutes, I flag down a waitress and ask her to check the restroom. My leg bounces, waiting for her to return, and fury fills me when she tells me Jade was seen leaving through the fire exit.

Now, as I drive home, anger consumes me. I'll punish that little ass of hers and remind her she needs to be my good girl.

The security gates open slowly, grating on my last nerve as my hands itch to mark her perfect skin, and my mind craves to see her.

Finally pulling up outside the mansion, I slam the car door and storm my way inside.

I rush up the stairs, waving off my security detail as I do.

My hand finds the handle to the door, but when I discover it's locked, my temper escalates.

"Jade, open this fucking door!" I boom.

Silence. My temple pulsates at the lack of acknowledgment. I'll tan her fucking ass for this.

"Jade. Open this fucking door before I smash it in!" I seethe.

Nothing.

With an almighty roar, I slam my body against the solid wood, sending it swinging from the hinges.

Guilt hits me in the chest, and my stomach sinks at the sound of her sobs. I push the guilt aside and allow the anger to consume me as I pull the bedsheet off her. She's showered and the thought pisses me off. She's washed away my scent, my touch, and in turn, she's washed away the blood that showed my possession of her.

Her tear-streaked face is on full display, and my cock hardens at the thought that she's crying for me. Will she cry so beautifully when I shove my cock inside her? When I fuck her so hard, she forgets any boy she's been with?

"Get out!" She points toward the door. "I don't want to speak to you, Tommy."

My body shakes in rage. How dare she tell me to leave? How dare she call me Tommy?

"Don't piss me off, little girl. You won't like the consequences," I warn while climbing onto the bed.

Her startled eyes widen.

"You slept with her." She exhales, tears streaking her pretty face.

I straddle her small body, reveling in how pliable she is below me.

"I did. I slept with a lot of them," I confirm as her lip wobbles. Swooping down, I tug the plump flesh into my mouth and give it a sharp bite, making her jolt.

Sitting back on my heels, I slowly unzip my pants.

"Tommy?"

"Stop with the fucking Tommy," I bite out. "You know damn well you like calling me Daddy."

She shakes her head from side to side as though rejecting it. Rejecting me. And fury rumbles inside me. "You're mine, little girl, and I'm yours. Now it's time for Daddy to show you." My cock weeps at the insinuation.

I push up her sundress.

She's flustered. "Tommy! I mean, Daddy. What are you doing?"

I smirk at her little slipup and how easily she falls back into the need for me to protect her. "I'm going to stretch your little cunt to fit me." She gasps in panic. "Then I'm going to fuck your little pussy raw."

Panic coats her face. "Wait."

I shake my head, refusing to listen, refusing to hold back any longer. I need to make her mine. Reassuring myself as much as her.

My cock drips onto her panties as I tug them to the side. I suck in a sharp breath of air at the sight of her bare pussy glistening for me. Her arousal fills my nostrils. Fuck, I can't wait to taste her again. To slide my tongue over her plump lips while nuzzling into her hole.

"Wait. Please."

I release my cock to use both hands to snap her panties from her hips, discarding the cotton material onto the floor. All the while, she makes disapproving noises I refuse to listen to.

Using my knees, I push her legs wider and drag my cock down her slit. The action makes my eyes roll to the back of my head. "Fuck, little girl. So good, all wet for Daddy."

"Wait. Please, Daddy. Wait." The urgency in her voice gives me pause, but I've no intention of stopping. Not now that I've seen her little hole dripping for me and know how her bare cunt feels against my skin.

"I've never. I haven't." Her cheeks glow as my eyes narrow on her, trying to figure out what she's saying.

In annoyance, I lunge forward, gripping her throat with both hands, and her lips tremble as I use my weight to pin her down. "I'm a virgin," she breathes out. A lone tear trailing down her face as her words finally register. My eyes close on their own as euphoria pumps through me. No other cock has been inside her. None. She'll only ever know mine. "I'm a virgin," she repeats. I snap my eyes open, trailing my tongue over her tear and up to her forehead, where I release a gentle kiss.

"Your daddy's going to fuck you now, little girl."

Moving one hand from her throat, I use it to drag my cock to her small hole, slowly pushing inside her tight little pussy.

The skin on my cock tightens as I inch farther inside. Her warmth encompasses me as her body struggles to accept me. "Let me in, little girl. Let Daddy fuck this little cunt."

"Oh god," she breathes out.

I trail kisses down her face and over the side of her neck, relishing in the tightness surrounding my cock.

"Fuck. Daddy's going to come inside you. You'd like that, wouldn't you? Filling your little pussy with Daddy's cum."

She gasps, her back arching as I push into her innocence. Her whole body is coiled tight with the intrusion, and her little moans of discomfort are the most incredible sounds I've ever heard; they make my balls ache with a feverish need to unload inside her.

"I'm . . . I'm not on birth control." Her words whoosh out of her lips on a whisper and fill my veins with determination. My body jolts with the enormity of hearing those words.

"We could have a baby of our own," I mumble in shock. This way, I'd always have a part of her, and she would have a part of me. She'd need me forever like I need her. Protection, control, and obsession surge through me, giving me no other option than to pull back and drive into her so hard she screams out as I pierce through her virginal cunt.

"That's it. You're Daddy's now. Daddy's going to put a baby in you, little girl."

I pull back again and slam inside her harder. Again, faster. I have an urge to watch the plump flesh of her tits bounce as I fuck her. Quickly, I remove my hand from her throat, and like a wild animal, I tear the fabric from her chest while my hips piston into her faster and faster, forcing the mattress to creak and the headboard to bang against the plastered wall.

I tear her tits from her bra before dipping my head to tug on her pebbled nipple. One, then the other.

My cock pulsates with each little breathy moan of pleasure or discomfort that leaves her.

"Daddy's going to fill you with a baby." I ram inside her. Slamming hard.

"Yes. Oh god, yes."

I pull back on my heels to watch my cock sink into her pussy. Fuck, it's the best thing I've ever seen, my thick cock stretching her pussy hole open. Pulling out, it's coated in her blood and innocence, and I have to clench my teeth to ward off my impending orgasm.

"Your shirt. Lose your shirt." Her hands come up to the buttons of my shirt.

Fire burns inside me at the thought of her needing me as much as I need her. "You want to see me? You want to see Daddy fuck you?" I knock her hands away, opting to tear it from me.

Her eyes fill with lust. "Look!" I grip her chin and point her head down toward where we're connected. Pulling my cock almost all the way out so she can see the blood coating it. "Can you see your blood on my cock?" She nods.

"It shows how your pussy is made for me." Her lips fall open and her pussy tightens unbelievably more around my cock. "This pussy is mine, little girl." Our eyes hold one another's hostage. "And I'm fucking yours!" I drive inside her on a roar, letting her know no other woman interests me. No other woman exists apart from her.

"Yours, Daddy." She convulses around my cock, and I allow myself to spill deep inside her, so fucking deep she has no choice but to accept my baby growing in her.

"Fuck. Daddy's giving you a baby." I pant as I fall forward onto my arms, resting directly above her head.

Her soft lips graze mine, my mouth opening to accept her tongue, and this time when my cock hardens, there's not a doubt in my mind that I'm making love to her.

She's forbidden.

She's innocent.

She's my little girl.

"Yours," she breathes out, admitting our feelings.

"Yours." I agree.

Chapter Thirteen

Tommy

She rests her head on my chest, drawing her fingertip over my tattoos, tracing them delicately while I stroke over her hair tenderly. It's a soothing act I've never participated in but something I crave to continue. Forever.

"I really need to pee." She giggles against me. Her soft breath flutters over my chest, and I squeeze her closer to me, not prepared to let her go just yet. Banding my arm around her waist, I tap her. "Straddle me. I want to see you." Slowly, she rises, looking like a little goddess as her teeth clamp into her lip, and she throws her leg over my muscular waist.

My gaze starts at the sparkling emeralds of her eyes and works down, following the pink flush of her cheeks under my scrutiny and over her chest to where her hair hides the precious swell of her tits. Using my fingers, I gently brush her hair over her shoulder, smoothing it and allowing her marked tits to be exposed to me. The bite marks littering her skin make my cock jump in a need to fill her. My little girl feels it too.

She rocks her pussy over my solid cock, and her eyes flutter closed when I take hold of her hips to help her grind down on me. "Mm, that's it. Rock your bloodied little cunt on me," I grit out.

Air whooshes from her lips as she moves faster while I let my palms explore the heavy weight of her tits, pulling at her nipples, pinching them roughly between my fingertips, the action making her press down harder while gyrating her little ass against me.

"That's it, be a good girl and come on Daddy's cock." The tip of my cock is pressed between us, and the precum hits my stomach as she uses me as her fuck toy. "My little girl is a slut. Aren't you?"

She doesn't answer me, so I slap her tit hard, making her eyes fly open.

"Ye-yes, Daddy." I move one of my hands, raising it behind her to bring it down against her soft flesh as I spank her little ass. The moment my palm touches her skin, she goes off like a rocket, letting out an almighty scream that rings in my ears. Her hands fall onto my chest to stabilize herself. Her low pants make me desperate for more from her, for everything.

"You're such a good girl, baby," I coo, tucking her hair behind her ear as she lifts her head to face me. Her whole face lights up at my words, loving the praise, and when she bites into her bottom lip with an element of shyness to it, my thick cock pulsates and precum squirts from the slit, making a sticky mess on my abs.

A mess I intend to add to.

"I really need to pee." She blushes, making my heart hammer with an urge to consume every part of her.

Giving her tits a final tweak, I move my hands to her hips and hold her forcefully, leaving no mistaking my words. "Go ahead." I grind my cock below her while watching her face for a reaction.

Her eyebrows narrow as she glances from my cock to my face, not yet registering the insinuation behind my words, so I stiffen my hands on her further, bruising her skin, no doubt. "Go ahead," I repeat.

"Da . . . Daddy?"

My eyes roll to the back of my head on her stuttered breath, and the innocence behind her tone is an aphrodisiac for my desire to dominate her.

Her body freezes as if realizing my intentions, and I snap my eyes open to witness it. "Go ahead," I coax once again, encouraging her to pee if necessary.

"I . . . I can't." She swallows shallowly and I revel in it. Her nervousness makes my cock jump, but the anticipation of such a forbidden act with my little girl has my veins filling with an obsessive power to feel her come apart above me in the most intimate of ways.

"You can." I move my hands to press down on her stomach, startling her. "And you will." I push down on her harder. "Piss on my cock, little girl." Her lips part in shock. "Do it. Let Daddy feel your warm piss on his cock. Make Daddy come, my beautiful little slut."

"Oh god!" She lifts her ass up slightly, and when I press down firmer, giving her no other option but to hover those pussy lips over the tip of my cock, the warmth of her piss hits me, my throat goes dry, and my body tightens with exhilaration as the flood of liquid leaves her body.

"Holy fuck!" My mouth falls open. "Jesus, Jade. That's it. Fuck, that's it." Her warmth engulfs the tip of my cock, and the force of her piss is a powerful pressure against the tip.

She whimpers, and her eyes flick back and forth from my face to her pussy as she pees, as though equally in shock and turned on but also uncomfortable with the action. "That's it, little girl." I praise, letting her know how much I'm enjoying the feel and control of her. "Piss on Daddy's cock."

"Ahhh." Her nails dig into my chest while she lets her piss flow from her in a short, steady stream, and when she stops, I line my dripping, aching cock up and slam inside her pussy hole, ignoring the wetness surrounding us.

Like a limp doll straddling my body, I power up into her, thrusting over and over again, making her tits sway and her head loll. "Fuck, that's it. Take it. Take my cock, you dirty little slut." I unleash on her, stretching her hole, and then I move one hand from her hip and give her ass a sharp slap, following it up swiftly with another, and another, each blow stronger than the last. "Beautiful little slut, pissing on Daddy."

"Oh god," she moans, clenching her pussy around me.

I bite into my bottom lip, embracing the force of my hips powering into her and loving how I use her lithe body to grind her down onto my abs. Each movement rubs against her little clit, and she mewls in response.

"Daddy, I'm . . ." Darting my hand out toward her throat, I press my fingers against her pulse. In response, her cunt grasps me firmer. Surging faster into her, I lean forward and spit at her face, sending her spiraling into the abyss, and my own euphoria takes me over. I follow behind her, and my vision darkens while my body floats. My cum unleashes in thick, sharp spurts, filling her cunt with my essence. I'm vaguely aware of my grip loosening and her body falling onto mine.

"I love you, Daddy," she whispers as I tuck her against me.

"I love you too, little girl."

Chapter Fourteen

Tommy

I gather the fruit onto the tray, along with freshly squeezed orange juice, and make my way upstairs. Pushing open her bedroom door, my heart skips a beat at her small body in the ridiculously frilly bedspread. My lip quirks up at the thought. Just what the hell was Jenna thinking decorating the room like this?

Her head pops up from the pillow and she sits up on her elbows, our eyes clashing. I watch in awe as her chest rises rapidly as if filled with trepidation. Then, when she eyes the tray with breakfast, her shoulders relax and her features soften, making me smile at how worried she was that I might have regretted last night.

How could I possibly regret it?

She imprinted on me. Left her mark so deep she's ingrained in me forever. And I hope for nothing more than it to scar my already tattered heart. An organ that once only beat for one but now beats for her too.

The bedsheet slips, exposing her milky tit, and when she moves to cover herself once again, I snap, "Leave it."

Her startled green eyes meet mine, but she nods delicately as I place the tray on the bed and sit beside it.

"Come here." I tap my knee for her to join me.

She bites into her lip. "I'm naked, Tommy."

I cluck my tongue. "Daddy in the bedroom, little girl," I chastise. "Come and sit on Daddy's lap and let me look after you."

Her throat works, and her eyes flash with vulnerability and intrigue as she nibbles into her bottom lip, making my cock throb at the sight. Slowly, she crawls from beneath the sheets and across the bed, making my body vibrate with arousal.

She's a fucking vision with her wavy brown locks hanging down toward her tits.

A low growl emits from my throat when she eases her perky little ass onto my lap. My eyes travel over her small, naked form, bare for the taking. Fuck, I could eat her whole. I drape an arm around her back, holding her in place. With a hand on her thigh, I nudge her legs open, earning a small gasp of surprise from her.

Dried blood coats the inside of her thighs, and I've never felt so positively primal in my entire life. My hand tightens on her in an obsessive, protective movement.

She glances down toward her pussy and blushes an identical shade of the crimson evidence of her stolen virginity.

"Fuck, you're beautiful when you blush, little girl." I nuzzle into her hair, breathing her in, then I place gentle kisses over her neck as I nudge her hair off her shoulder, leaving her soft skin exposed for me to mark further.

"Daddy," she breathes out, making my cock stiffen

against my boxers, which she feels, judging by the way she rocks against it.

I place another kiss on her neck and pick up a strawberry, bringing it to her lips. She bites into it, the juice running from her mouth, making her giggle. I turn her face and drag my tongue over her chin, lapping up the remnants before repeating the action with another strawberry and another. "Good girl."

Widening my legs, it forces hers to widen, too, allowing me access to her pussy. Picking up another strawberry, I dip it between her thighs and circle her small, swollen hole before pushing it inside. She jumps at the slight intrusion, and she grips my arm, making me laugh. "Be a good girl and let Daddy feed you."

She turns her head toward me, and her eyes widen in horror. I smirk in response to her shocked expression. "Wait, you can't be serious?"

My lip tips up. "Deadly. Now be a good girl and open up." She clamps her lips shut, and her eyes bug out further. My cock swells excruciatingly more at the thought of forcing her. She gives her head a small shake, refusing my request. "You want Daddy to force you, little girl?" The pulse in her neck races, her skin heats, and her breathing becomes stuttered. "My little girl likes the thought of Daddy punishing her, doesn't she?" Her pupils dilate. "Be a good girl and open up, then Daddy will clean you up with his tongue." She lets out a whimper and tries to squeeze her thighs together, and her arousal is now evident on my leg. Slowly, she opens her mouth, allowing me to feed her the strawberry with her pussy juice on it. "That's our cum on there, little girl. You're tasting us both. Don't we taste sweet together?"

"Mmm," she moans around the strawberry before

sucking my digit into her mouth, where she flicks her tongue over the tip.

My cock throbs and my balls ache. "Fuck!" I sink my teeth into her neck and tug sharply, letting her know how much she affects me.

My cock throbs at the sight of her. Unable to take it anymore, I pick her up and throw her onto the mattress while I drop to my knees. Barely giving her a chance to sit up, I pull her ass to the edge of the bed and widen her legs, draping them over my shoulders while my head dips down to her plump pussy lips.

"Fuck, you're all swollen." I groan and place a gentle kiss against her pussy. Then, I use my tongue to show her how much I care. I caress it, flicking my tongue over her bud, then peppering her with loving, soft kisses. "Daddy's going to clean up our mess." I lift my gaze to watch her. When her tongue darts out over her lip, I lose all coherent thoughts. Dipping my head, I nuzzle into her stained thighs and breathe in her arousal. "You smell so edible, painted in our cum, little girl."

She moans, grabbing the sheet as I lick and suck away her blood, all while my cock leaks and I groan in ecstasy against her. I spread her folds, embracing the wetness between them and the taste of her copper on my tongue. Her cries of pleasure spur me on, but I'm determined to finish my feast before I finish in my boxers.

"Daddy, it's good. It's so good," she mumbles. "Please don't stop." I place my hands beneath her ass and squeeze her cheeks tightly.

"Mmm," I growl into her, pushing my face hard against her so she can rub her little cunt against it.

"More, Daddy." She pants, grinding her pussy into my

face, covering it in her juices. Fuck, that's hot. Her bare little cunt thrusting up for her daddy to please.

"Oh god."

"Take what you need, little girl. Take it from Daddy."

I latch on to her clit, sucking it into my mouth while rubbing the scruff of my face against her pussy, allowing her the friction to fuck me. To take what she needs as she writhes under my control.

"Ahhh, Daddy." She groans while moving her hand to dig her nails into my scalp, all while fucking my face mercilessly.

She throws her head back with a scream, and before she can come down from her orgasm, I stand, tug down my boxers, kick them to the side, and pull her legs up toward my shoulders. I drive my cock into her pussy hole, hissing with how tight it is around me.

"Fuck, little girl. So tight around Daddy's cock." I bite into the side of my cheek. "So fucking tight." I slam inside her. "Let Daddy stretch it. Stretch this little hole for Daddy to fill."

"Yes, oh god, yes please." *Slam.*

I pound inside her relentlessly, and she lies there, letting me. Letting me use her as my little fuck doll. "That's it, let Daddy use this tight little cunt."

Her warm cunt holds my cock like a clamp, making me want to come. "Fuck, your pussy is strangling my cock, little girl." I drive into her harder. Deeper.

"Oh god. It hurts." She mewls.

My cock spurts at her pained words. "That's Daddy's cock stretching you." I grind my jaw as my orgasm approaches far quicker than I'd anticipated. But where she's concerned, I don't seem to be able to control my urges.

"Be a big girl and take it." *Thrust.* "Take all my fucking

cock." *Slam.* "Let me fill you with my cum, little girl."

"Yes, yes, please," she pants out, begging as I grip her thighs with such force she'll bruise. I drive into her harder and harder. Faster and faster.

"I might get pregnant. I-I'm not on birth control, Daddy."

"Fuck yes. Daddy wants to put a baby in you." *Slam.* She moans as I grind my hips against her, and her pussy clenches at the motion.

"Fuck yes. That's it, make Daddy come. Let Daddy fill you with our baby."

She arches her back and squeezes my cock again. "Fuck, Jade. I'm . . ."

Her mouth parts and air whooshes from her lips as her body locks up tight and I finally give in to my orgasm. My cock swells, and I allow it to release with a hard thrust as deep as possible. I hold her tight in my hands, continuously pumping my cock inside her, determined for my cum to take form and create a life connecting us together.

Forever.

The strength of my orgasm sends me falling onto her, making my lips crash against hers in a heady concoction of possession, power, and passion.

The embers sparking once again and fire igniting in sloppy, desperate kisses filled with the strength I feel for her.

I pull back, breathless, my eyes full of love for my girl. "You're so beautiful, little girl. So fucking beautiful." I kiss her again as her fingers tangle in the hair at the nape of my neck, and my cock swells as she widens her legs to accept my body, then wraps them around my waist as I rock into her.

She accepts my cum, and, ultimately, my baby too.

Chapter Fifteen

Jade

We lie in bed, completely satiated. My chin rests on his chest as I trace over his tattoos with the tip of my finger, my aching, bruised body sprawled over his solid one. "Have you always had women call you Daddy in the bedroom?"

He lifts his head to stare down at me, and his dark eyes narrow on mine. Raising his hand, he tucks my hair behind my ear before trailing his knuckles tenderly down my cheek. "Never."

I swallow back the emotion clogging my throat. This whole dynamic is as new for him as it is for me, and I couldn't be any more elated, but I try not to show it.

"Do you like that?" he asks, tilting his head to the side. "That you're the first girl without experience that I've fucked? The first girl I let call me Daddy?" He licks his lips and swallows. "My first little girl."

I nod gingerly because, if truth be told, it fills me with a sense of security I've never felt before now. It makes me feel wanted. Needed. Protected.

"My cock is constantly hard for you, Jade." He lifts his hips to rub his hard cock against me for emphasis. "You've become my little obsession. The cure to my addiction." He swallows thickly and lowers his voice. "But it scares me." He admits meekly.

I move to sit beside him. Tucking my legs under me, I perch my ass on them, and he tilts his head against my lap for me to run my fingers through his thick, dark hair. His Adam's apple slides up and down his throat before he finally speaks. "I'm scared I won't be able to come back from this addiction. That I'll become so obsessed that when you end it, it'll destroy me. I won't survive the withdrawal." His eyes stay fixed on mine, and the vulnerability in them has my hammering heart aching at his words and my stomach sinking. His words hit me with such force they send a brutal tremor through my body. How could he think I'd discard him so easily? How can he not see I'm as addicted as him?

That we're both addicts in this relationship.

How ironic that we're both also the cure.

"I won't ever leave you, Tommy."

Our eyes remain locked.

"You're mine," I tell him with certainty. "You'll always be my daddy."

Tommy

I send a message for Jade to come to my office, knowing full well my father will be calling at any moment. My excited cock rubs against my belt at the thought.

She knocks on the door, making me grin like a bastard as my plan comes together.

"Come in." I try to hide the enthusiasm behind my voice and instead shuffle papers on my desk, feigning work.

"Is everything okay?" She furrows her brows.

Roaming my eyes over her summer dress, I groan in the back of my throat at how innocent she looks. Jesus, she couldn't be any more opposite of the women I normally go for.

It's like she's heaven sent. An angel sent straight into the devil's lair.

"I miss you, that's all."

She blushes at my words, and although they're not a lie, they're not what brings her here right now.

I hold out my hand, and when her palm slips into mine so willingly, it sends a shot of electricity through me, landing heavily in my balls. Picking her up by her delicate hips, I perch her ass on the edge of the desk, and she giggles in glee, swiping a hand at my chest playfully. "You only saw me this morning."

"Mmm, I know." I pepper kisses over her covered stomach, making my cock pulsate as I imagine her swollen with my baby. Her fingers find my hair as I melt into her and her into me.

As if on cue, my phone rings, vibrating against the wooden desk. I growl in annoyance at having to disconnect from her.

I press the button to answer. "Tommy, how are things?" My father's voice fills the air, startling Jade, but then she freezes.

"Fine." I smirk as I lift her dress up to her hips. She tries to shove it back down, but I force it up and lift my eyes to meet hers, sending her a warning glare to comply. The fire behind my stare makes her swallow, and I give her a swift nod as she gives up and relaxes, allowing me to raise her dress.

Lowering my head, I place a gentle kiss over her mound, making her breathe out a low, contented sigh. Then I trail my finger over her innocent cotton panties, and she sucks in a sharp breath. Then I take the opportunity to push them aside and her hands tighten on the edge of the desk.

"And how's Jade?"

She stills at the mention of her name.

Using a finger, I swipe it up and down her slit, then I dip it into her wet pussy. She tries to close her legs, so I scoot the chair forward, forcing myself between them, and then give her a chastising glance through narrowed eyes.

"You mean my daughter?" I snipe out. Pissed at the sound of her name on his traitorous lips.

I swipe my tongue over her folds, breathing her in, then

dip it into her hole and swirl it around, gathering our cum. I swallow it down greedily with a groan. She brings her hand to her mouth to stifle her own moan of approval, and I smile into her, relishing her scent and taste. The sweetness on my tongue is a reminder of our baby-making.

The fact she allows me to fuck her bare, to spill inside her virginal cunt, drives me wild to the point of insanity.

My father exhales loudly. "Right. Your stepdaughter. How is she?" His tone is clipped as if pissed at my sudden interest in her.

"Fine," I snipe back, annoyed he's taking me away from eating her pussy. She pushes into my face as she rests back on her elbows, now embracing what I'm doing to her. Accepting the pleasure I'm gifting her.

Quickly moving, I lean up and whisper in her ear, "Play with your tits. Show Daddy your tits while you fuck my face. Roll those little nipples for me." The tip of my cock leaks uncontrollably, and her breathing escalates, making me smile in glee as I duck back down to her needy pussy.

"Has she mentioned college to you?"

I lap at her juices, watching her lower the straps of her dress, and she scoops her tits out of her bra, letting them fall over the lace fabric. Fuck, her perfect nipples are peaked, begging to be sucked and played with. Begging for me to taste.

"Mmm," she moans.

The forbiddance of the situation has more precum pouring into my boxers as she grinds against my face like the needy girl she is. Pushing a finger into her tight hole, I wonder how the fuck I ever got my cock in her; she's so small. I grunt in approval as I work my finger in and out of her slickness.

"Well, has she?" he spits out.

I stop my movements and snap my head up, and her body sags against the desk.

"What?"

"Has she mentioned college yet?"

Pressing my face back into her pussy, I nibble around her clit. "No," I breathe out from between her trembling thighs.

He sighs heavily. "She needs to choose a college. She hasn't chosen one yet."

"Mm," she moans loudly when I sink two fingers deep inside her, stretching her and curling them to press on her G-spot. It forces her ass up off the desk as she rides them, and her chest rises faster and faster as she chases her orgasm.

"Jade? Are you there?" my father snaps out, as though growing aggravated with the constant pauses in conversation.

"Yes," she pants out, grinding her pussy into my face.

"Are you working out or something?" he quizzes, making me chuckle.

She squeezes her tit as she arches her back, and I withdraw my face and fingers at the same time, putting a sudden stop to her impending orgasm.

There's a pregnant pause before she comes to her senses and clears her throat. "Yes, Mr. Marino. I'm working out." I grin back at her while she glares back at me. Leaning over her, I once again whisper in her ear, "Take me out." I nod down toward my granite cock. She shakes her head, and I clench my jaw in frustration. I wrap my hand around her neck and squeeze, making her eyes bulge. "Take me fucking out. Otherwise, I'll ram my cock in your throat while he listens." Her eyes flare in panic.

"I . . . I've never," she whispers on a swallow.

Fuck, is she telling me she's never touched a cock before? I think back over our limited time together, and sure enough, her hand has never grasped my cock. The fact that she's never held one makes me desperate to pump into her small hand like a ruthless animal. Like the addict I am.

I gift her a reassuring nod as she slides off the edge of the desk. Pointing to my lap, she climbs onto it without protest.

"Have you chosen a college yet, Jade?" my father asks, his voice laced with concern.

Concern which he has no place having, and the thought makes me pissed.

She unbuckles my belt and fumbles with my zipper.

Just the stroke of her soft hand against my cock has me harder than being physically touched by anyone before. It's like nobody else exists but her as I melt into her touch.

Her hand slides down my velvety shaft, and my cock pulsates beneath her, my hips driving up in desperation. She rests her body against my chest as she pumps me up and down, forcing me to hiss between my teeth at the contact. Somehow, I resist the urge to throw her down on the desk and fuck her like a crazed man.

I move the hair from off her shoulders, exposing her bite mark, while I whisper in her ear, "Such a good girl for Daddy. Pumping his thick cock in her small hand."

Her thighs clench together, and I groan at how much she needs me to fill her.

Using my free hand, I circle her nipple between my fingers, plucking it while she toys with my balls. Fuck, it feels incredible. Liquid heat spurts out of the tip of my cock, giving her lubricant to play with as she slides her hand back up.

"A college, Jade. Did you choose one yet?" My father's

pissed-off voice comes over the speaker, causing her to jolt and her hand to pause. I clench my teeth in response to his intrusion, stopping what is quite literally the most incredible hand job of my entire life.

"No," she breathes out irritably, her jaw setting as though frustrated at the topic of conversation.

I tap her thigh and whisper to her, "Climb on." I nod down toward my cock, making her suck in a sharp breath, and her eyes dart to me, then away in uncertainty.

"Jade," I grind out at her lack of movement.

"Exactly. You need to listen to your stepfather, Jade, and think about your future." My father inadvertently agrees with me, making her stifle a smile by biting her teeth into her bottom lip adorably.

I tap her thigh again and glare at her in warning.

When she slowly throws her leg over my hip to straddle me, I growl while holding my cock in position before slamming her down onto it—all the way to the fucking hilt. My eyeballs roll to the back of my head as my cock pulses against the stretch of her pussy while her mouth falls open in a silent scream. Fuck yes.

I lift her again and slam her down. "Fuck, little girl." She whimpers as I drive up into her. Her fingernails dig into my shirt as she grasps my shoulders, allowing me to control her small body like a puppet on a string.

"Dirty fucking slut, letting Daddy fuck you." I hiss and bite into her neck.

"Oh god." She holds my head against her, pulling my hair as I thrust my cock deep inside her while slamming her up and down on my cock.

"Mmm, please," she moans in little, short, sharp gasps.

"Is everything okay over there?" My father's voice

becomes white noise as I make it my mission to fill my little girl with my cum.

My father chuckles to himself. "Is he working you hard?"

"Mmm, so hard," she moans, making me smile against her skin.

Pleasure shoots through my balls as I stifle a groan against the delicate flesh of her neck.

"Well, you two enjoy yourselves. And maybe come up with a plan for college?" my father asks.

Taking a hand from her hip, I circle her needy clit, determined to make her come with me. Her pussy clenches, strangling my cock and making it almost impossible to move inside her. Using all my force, I slam as deep as possible, willing my seed to take shape.

"Oh, Daddy!"

I slam my hand over her mouth, fumbling with the cell to cut the call as I come balls deep in my stepdaughter.

"Fuck, little girl. You take Daddy's cock so good."

Chapter Sixteen

Jade

Ellie swirls her finger around her milkshake, her eyes not leaving mine. "You're fucking him, aren't you?"

My heart hammers in my chest, and tears fill my eyes as I swallow back the emotion threatening to spill over.

She stretches her hand over the table to take hold of mine, then glances around the diner and lowers her voice. "Hey, it's okay. If I had a hot daddy like that, I'd fuck him too." I can feel the heat creeping over my neck at her words, reminding me of how I call him Daddy.

"Oh god. You call him Daddy, don't you?" Her playful smile covers her face, and her eyebrows dance in excitement. Then she lets out a shrieking noise, bouncing her ass on the bench while clapping her hands together like an excitable child. I roll my eyes at her childish antics.

Ellie has always been the playful, confident one, while I have always been levelheaded, with a touch of feistiness brought on by insecurity.

"Did he pop your cherry?" She grins at me, her eyes

lighting up. "Please tell me he's big and knows what he's doing?"

I laugh while picking at the nachos. "He's big and knows what he's doing," I admit, smirking back at her.

"Ugh, I knew it. You're so lucky." Ellie slumps back against the bench.

"You can't tell anyone." I point my nacho at her, making her roll her eyes at me this time.

"Duh, of course not."

Exhaling heavily, I admit for the first time how I feel about my future. "I really don't want to go to college."

Ellie's eyes fill with sympathy. "You don't have to. Just because his father wants you to doesn't mean you have to do anything."

"He's been so good to me, though. He even offered to pay for my tutoring and accommodations."

"Well, what do you want?" She sits back and crosses her arms over her chest, making me giggle at how serious she's acting.

I pop another nacho in my mouth. "I want to continue working at the bakery."

"And then what?"

Sighing, I feel the aggravation rising in me. "Why does there have to be more? Why can't I just be happy baking?"

"Like the perfect little housewife? I can see it now. Baking fresh cookies for the kids." I know she's mocking me, but my heart releases a pang at her jest. Because, deep down in my heart, there's nothing I want more than a family. A healthy, comforting family with a life that allows me to care for them. Something I never had but always longed for.

"Does Daddy know you work at the bakery?"

My jaw tightens at the word. "Don't call him that," I snap.

She chokes on a laugh, holding her hands up in defense, which makes my lips tip up into a reassuring smile.

"Yes, he knows, and he wasn't happy about it."

"Mmm. Didn't think he would be. Have you spoken to him about it?"

"No, he wanted me to quit, but I have a shift on Saturday. I'll tell him I'm going before I leave."

"Something tells me Tommy Marino isn't going to be so happy about his girl working."

I lift my gaze to hers. "I'm not his girl." Even saying the words stings. It's on the tip of my tongue to tell her I'm his little girl, but I bite my tongue.

My phone buzzes on the table, and "Daddy" flashes on the screen.

Flicking open the message, warmth fills me at his words.

Daddy: I miss you.

Me: I miss you too.

Daddy: I'm going out. But I won't be long.

Me: Okay. I'll be home soon anyway.

Daddy: I like that you call it home.

I swoon at his words, loving how I call it home too.

Me: Me too.

Daddy: I'm going to drive my cock home later. Right into you.

I scoff with a giggle, making Ellie raise an eyebrow in my direction, but I shake my head, refusing to divulge my private life any further. I've already overstepped today; I need to speak to Tommy before I go too far.

Daddy: Rafael might swing by later, he needs to collect some paperwork.

Me: Okay. Can I bring Ellie home for a while?

Daddy: Of course. You don't need to ask. It's your home too, Jade.

Daddy: No boys.

I grin back at the phone, loving how possessive he is of me.

Me: You were pissed last time I had guests.

Daddy: That was different, and you know it. You had your tits out.

My mouth falls open.

Daddy: Right now, I'm imagining your mouth open and my cock stuffing it.

Me: I have no words.

Daddy: Yes, you do. Daddy will suffice.

Me: Yes, Daddy.

Me: Stuff my mouth with your cock.

Daddy: Jesus. I'm as hard as a fucking rock again.

I smile as I take a drink of my milkshake, imagining him walking around with his hard cock.

Daddy: I'll punish you later.

Me: Yes, Daddy.

Daddy: Good girl.

Smiling down at my phone, I place it in my purse.

"Fancy coming back to my house for a while? Tommy is out."

Ellie throws down her straw. "Damn, and I wanted to check out Daddy Tommy's package." She sticks her tongue out at me, making me laugh as we gather our shopping bags.

Excitement fills me as we head out the door toward home.

Finally, a place where I can be myself.

Tommy

Laughter fills the air as I walk into my home, and I breathe in the sound.

For the first time in years, I couldn't wait to return here.

I know Jade thinks I don't work, but occasionally, I have to oversee things. So when my father needed files sent over from his office, he called me. Which is rare, given I'm usually the last person he would ever ask to do anything for him. But his asking me out of the blue made it easier for me to relent and do it. Given he gave up asking me to help years ago.

When Jenna noticed me, she followed me into my father's office like a guard dog protecting its territory. My jaw clenched in annoyance as she watched over me while I transferred the files and emailed them over to him. Then she rounded his desk and fell to her knees, making my balls shrivel up and my body shake, threatening to expel the contents.

"What do you think you are doing?" I gritted out.

She threw her hair over her shoulder and licked her lips in a manner that could have been deemed seductive.

"I'm going to give you a blow job." Her nails dug into my thighs, and I swiped her grabby hands away from me.

"Like fuck you are!" I spat out.

I pushed back in my chair to stand, heading toward the door before she could follow.

"Tommy, wait. You can come on my face, just how you like it."

My eyes bugged out. The only place I want my cum is inside my woman, filling her with my child.

"Whatever this was"—I waved my hand around in her direction while trying to keep the look of disgust off my face —"is over. I'm a taken man."

Her mouth fell open. And where normally I'd have stuffed it until she choked, I really couldn't think of anything I'd like less.

Not when I have my girl waiting for me at home.

<hr>

A loud squeal makes my step stutter and I turn my head to listen to the sound. "Three, two, one. I'm coming to find you, Oliver."

My nephew's laughter fills the foyer, and I can't help but smile at the sound. When he comes skidding across the marble floor in front of me, I'm stunned by how much he's grown. Guilt floods me. Have I become so detached that the last I remember him, he was crawling? He makes a lame attempt to hide behind my legs, and I laugh out loud at his innocence.

Jade's friend Ellie comes rushing into the foyer but ignores me as she feigns knowing where Oliver is hiding. I stand stoically still, playing along.

The moment Jade comes into view, my heart races and

our eyes lock as a magnetic force pulls us together. She smiles softly, and I return it without thought.

"There you are!" Ellie squeals while lifting Oliver into her arms, and she tickles him, making him giggle in glee as his small legs kick out. "I got you!" she shrieks. The sound makes me and Jade jolt out of our lust-filled gaze.

My brother watches, leaning against the doorframe with his dark eyes trained on Ellie and his son. I know the wistful look in his eyes because it mirrors mine. My hands flex, desperate to pull Jade into my arms and show her how much I missed her today.

"Did you run into Jenna at the office?" Rafael asks, his dark gaze now focused on me. He glances toward Jade, and I can't help but feel something is off. I don't miss Jade's flinch at the use of Jenna's name, either.

"Yes," I bite out. Pissed he's bringing her up in Jade's presence, he doesn't realize the enormity of my anger.

His lip twitches. If his son wasn't in proximity, I'd put a fist to his cocky face.

"And?" he questions. Once again, it makes me wonder where he's going with this.

"And nothing." I shrug nonchalantly.

He drags a finger over his lip as he studies me, and I fucking hate it. Instead, I choose to change the subject.

"How's the hunt for the nanny going?"

I'm not interested in his quest to find the perfect mother figure for his son. Not when he chose such a poor excuse of a mother for him in the first place.

To be fair, he got little say in it, much like me. But he accepted it, the Mafia life. Embraced it even.

His eyebrows lift in surprise at me knowing about this shit. Honestly, I'm surprised too, but when you have a housekeeper that talks more about my family than I do, some of that shit is bound to sink into my head, no matter how uninterested I appear.

"I think I just found a new nanny." He nods in Ellie's direction, making me glare back at him. He throws his head back with a roaring laugh and the girls turn their attention in our direction.

My brother pushes off the wall. "Come on, Oliver, time to go home."

Oliver makes a grumbling noise as Ellie lowers him to the floor. Disappointment is also clear on her face. "We're taking Ellie home, don't worry." He smirks as he heads toward the door.

"Oh, erm." Ellie fidgets on the spot. "I guess I'll speak to you tomorrow, Jade?"

"Sure," Jade confirms as Ellie follows my brother and nephew through the door.

As soon as the door closes behind them, she turns toward me. "Did you miss me, Daddy?" She drags her tongue over her lip.

"Get the fuck over here and suck me off. I want to see my little girl on her knees for me."

Jade

"Get the fuck over here and suck me off. I want to see my little girl on her knees for me." As soon as he says those words, wetness fills my panties and I move without encouragement.

Walking toward him, our eyes hold one another hostage, and I give an extra sway to my hips. His eyes flick down toward my tits but then quickly snap back up to meet mine.

Standing foot to foot, I can feel the tension radiating from him. His muscles are coiled tight beneath his shirt as though he's fighting with himself.

Slowly, I lower myself to my knees, our eyes remaining connected.

Tommy's hands scramble to open his belt, as though desperate, and his Adam's apple slides down his throat when he lowers his zipper and still his eyes are trained on me. He pulls his thick cock from his boxers and gives it a couple of rough pulls before slapping it against my cheek, making me startle in shock. "Open." He hits my cheek with his cock again.

Watching his pupils darken and dilate, along with the firm grip on his cock, makes me want to please him. I open my mouth wide, expecting his cock to fill it, but then he places his thumb on my teeth and his fingers press on my chin, drawing it open farther while he tips my head back, then leans over me. A noise rumbles from the back of his throat, then I feel the wetness of his spittle dropping into my mouth. "Such a good little whore for Daddy."

My body vibrates under his approval, and my panties cling to my pussy. One hand moves to my throat and grips it tightly. "Daddy's going to choke you with his cock, little girl, and when I fill your little whore mouth, you're going to thank Daddy. Do you understand?"

I gift him with a nod, my mouth still open. I'm already struggling to breathe in the position I'm in with his hand clasped around my throat. "Swallow my spit." As I try to do as he asks and swallow against his hand, his fingers tighten more and a growl from his chest vibrates between us, filling the air with sheer domination.

He tilts my head up slightly, allowing our eyes to reconnect, then with his free hand, he places the tip of his cock on my tongue, setting it there with a smirk on his handsome face.

Weaving his fingers through my hair, he grips it with a sharp pinch before he plunges his cock forward with no warning. My hands scramble against his thighs in shock at the instant intrusion filling my mouth. Desperately, I try to push him away, but he ignores me, holding my head in place with his hand in my hair, giving me no option but to accept him.

"Fuck, yes. Fight me, little girl. Fight your daddy feeding you his cock." His hips work quicker, harder, slamming against my face as I struggle to breathe. His thick cock fills my mouth as I choke and splutter, tears flowing and running down my face, my heart racing in panic.

"Fuck yes, cry for Daddy."

Glancing up through tear-filled eyes, the look of pure ecstasy on Tommy's face makes me whimper in submission, and amazement coats his features as he stares down at me in awe. His lips are parted as he works his cock in and out of my mouth, and admiration flows from his eyes. His fingers on my throat twitch, then tighten.

"Fuck, you're incredible for Daddy. Fucking beautiful little girl." I moan around his cock, making it jump against the back of my throat. He slows his movements, and instantly, I worry I'm not good enough. "You want to taste Daddy, don't you?"

I blink, trying to tell him how much I want his cum to fill my mouth. "Good girl, good girl," he coos before going back to slamming inside me. "Fuck, you're going to make me come." His grip tightens as he works quicker and quicker, using my head as an anchor while he plunders my mouth. "Jesus. Fuck yes, Daddy's whore." His cock swells and the veins on his forearms tighten as I lick around his cock. My chest heaves as I struggle to breathe through my nose, but I try to concentrate on that as I lap around his cock, ignoring the mess slipping from my lips. He hits the back of my throat again and tightens his grip on my neck. "Fuck, here it is . . ." His mouth falls open and his eyes widen in what appears to be shock when his cock spurts ropes and ropes of his warm, salty cum into my mouth. It flows from my lips as I struggle to swallow it all down.

"Fuck." He exhales a deep breath and his movements steadily slow down.

With another deep breath, he slips his cock from me, then trails his thumb along my lower lip. "My beautiful little girl."

My heart soars with love at the longing behind his eyes and the tenderness of his touch after his brutal use of me.

Chapter Seventeen

Jade

Tommy sits behind me in the bathtub, washing my hair. His fingers work my scalp in a soothing motion that makes me want to purr like a content kitten. My whole body is lax under his talented fingers.

My mind whirls over this afternoon. The way Rafael looked at Ellie reminds me of how Tommy looks at me.

Like forbidden fruit he's desperate to taste.

I've met Rafael and his family at multiple events, so Oliver remembered who I was easily enough, but the usual shy little boy came out of his shell for my best friend—something that Rafael noticed quickly too.

While I know little about him, I know he's married. An arranged marriage, much like my mother's to Tommy. But unlike theirs, Rafael's would have been with the intention of a Mafia alliance as opposed to the business transaction my mother's was.

When Rafael mentioned Jenna, my whole body stilled.

The thoughts of him with that woman made me want to go on a violent rampage filled with grief.

I listened to their conversation and witnessed the confidence behind Tommy's voice, enough to feel satisfied that he hadn't touched her. I've never felt jealousy like that, and it made me realize how much I want us to work.

"I didn't touch her." He places a kiss on my shoulder as if hearing my thoughts. His lips send a thousand goose bumps trailing over my body. "I just wanted you to know. I didn't touch her." His voice is soft, so low I almost miss it.

But hearing him admit he didn't fuck her makes me bask in the hope of a future with him.

"I don't want to go to college," I admit, hating how vulnerable I sound.

Another kiss is rewarded, this one to my shoulder. "Then don't. I'll take care of you." Another kiss as I melt against him. "I want to take care of you. You can be anything you want to be, Jade, as long as I'm by your side when you do it." A contented sound leaves me, and he smiles against my shoulder, where he licks my bare skin all the way up toward my ear, where he gives it a quick nip, once again igniting the embers simmering inside me.

Tommy

"Is that what you like to hear, little girl? How Daddy will look after what's his?"

She spins in the water to face me. "And how do you think he's going to do that?" She sighs heavily like she has the weight of the world on her shoulders, which I hate. "You don't work, Tommy."

Annoyance builds inside me. Not at her words but at the position I've allowed myself to get into. Exhaling, my shoulders drop, and I'm finally able to admit, "You're right. I need to speak with my father. Figure something out." I tuck her wet hair behind her ear, focusing on the look of admiration in her eyes. "I want to do better. For you. For both of us. I want you, little girl."

Hope flickers on her face before it's quickly dispelled, making my spine straighten with tension. "But you don't want to be in the Mafia," she adds.

I shake my head. "Wrong. I didn't want to work with my father because I was punishing him. I don't care about my past anymore, Jade. The only thing I care about is you." Our eyes remain locked as I tell her the truth. "My future."

Her lips clash with mine, and I open my mouth willingly, our kiss becoming passionate and desperate. Her nails claw into my back, leaving scratches, and I hiss in approval while I bite into her lip. Each of us trying to battle the other for control. I pull her back by her hips, severing our connection, and her bruised lips part, her eyes heavy with lust.

"You're going to spin around on your hands and knees while I fuck you so fucking hard from behind you'll have no choice but to crawl around."

Her emerald eyes flare with arousal, making my hard cock flex against my stomach.

Slowly, she turns before lowering herself onto her elbows and knees. Her face is only an inch above the water, her tits submerged. Fuck me, that's hot.

Fire builds inside me, my little girl willingly handing herself over for me to use as I see fit. Taking one of the bottles from beside the bath, I move onto my knees behind her, squeezing some of the bath oil into my hands. I rub them together, then roughly knead her ass cheeks while watching her juicy little pussy drip with arousal. "Fuck, little girl, your ass needs fucking." She stills slightly, making me chuckle. "Not yet, not when I want my cum to fill you with my baby."

She drops her head. "Oh god, Daddy."

"That's right, moan for me, little girl."

I drag two fingers through her slick folds, bringing them around her ass, teasingly circling her tight hole with the tips of my fingers.

"Mmm, so good," she pants.

Moving my hand, I gently rub her clit, and when she grinds down on me, I give her ass a punishing slap, and she yelps in response.

"You're going to be my slut, little girl. You're going to let Daddy use you. Isn't that right?"

Our heavy breathing fills the bathroom.

"Yes, Daddy."

"Such a good girl," I coo while wrapping her wet hair around my fist like a rein. I tug it back brutally, making her head dart up and her throat stretch. She winces, and at that point, I line up my cock and slam into her tight, little pussy, relishing in the sound of her shocked gasp slipping from her lips.

"That's right, Daddy gets to do whatever he wants to you." I pull back and slam in harder, the water splashing over the edge of the tub and flooding the floor.

"Take it all, little girl." Drawing out to the tip of my cock, I surge forward with power behind each thrust, gripping her hair to force her in place, giving her no option but to take it. "That's it—" I grit my teeth. "Good fucking girl."

She slides in the tub and tries to dip her head down. My balls throb and draw up at the idea of submerging her. "Fuck yes," I choke out.

Splaying my fingers open on the back of her head with her hair still wrapped around me, I lean over her, applying pressure on her back. She bends beneath me while I ride her. "Good slut."

"Oh god!"

I shove her head under the water, her pussy clenches and her body fights against me, but I pin her in place, ramming my cock deeper on each drive of my hips. "Good slut," I hiss.

Then I tug her head up with a pull of her hair. She gasps for air, spluttering water from her mouth. She takes another deep breath and I allow it. "Daddy's washing all the dirt away." Her pussy clenches on my words.

"Again, little girl." I force her head below the water, relishing the panic of her body thrashing around as I drive into her. I move a hand beneath her and into the water, pressing hard against her clit, causing her pussy to clench. But I refuse to allow it. Not yet.

I stop and tug her up again to resurface.

Her heavy pants and gasps for breath make my balls draw up. "Daddy," she cries.

I pull out, slamming deep inside her. "Don't tell me to fucking stop." I slam into her. "I'm not stopping." I'm not sure who I'm trying to convince more, her or me. She tries to shake her head, but I refuse to acknowledge it. Every muscle is coiled tight with tension, with need, warding off my impending orgasm. Desperately fighting to keep it at bay.

"Daddy's going to drown you, little girl."

Once again, I shove her head down, and pleasure builds inside me at how accepting she is of her fate this time.

"But don't worry, Daddy will save you."

I grind my teeth, then bite into my lip as my orgasm approaches. Pulling her up once again for more air before just as quickly pushing her back under, her body stiffens, and I take pity on her when the head of my cock swells.

Yanking her all the way up so that her back slams hard against my chest, I slap my palm against her clit punishingly. She tightens in pleasure, and my jaw drops, lax as our orgasms clash and our bodies burn together in an explosion so prolific, we'll be scarred forever.

Chapter Eighteen

Jade

Tommy carried my spent body out of the tub last night while whispering loving, tender words as he wrapped me in a fluffy towel and took me into my bedroom.

Sitting on the edge of my bed, he cradled me in his arms while he patted me dry, then maneuvered to lay me on my stomach while he straddled my back and gently brushed out the knots in my damp hair. Then he placed cream on the bite marks of my skin.

His hard length brushed against me with each movement, and while I wouldn't have minded if he had slid back inside me again, I really wouldn't have been an active participant either. My body was far too tired and achy to be active.

He showered me in appreciative kisses, telling me, "You're such a good girl for Daddy. You're all nice and clean now, little girl."

Then he rolled onto his side, covering us with the obnoxious frilly pink comforter that just so happens to be growing on me while throwing a protective arm over me, holding me in place.

"Good night, little girl," he whispered into the room.

Opening my eyes, I glance at the nightstand clock and internally groan when I realize it's almost noon, surprised that Tommy let me sleep in so late.

Stretching my body, I grimace at the feeling of being bruised. Even my scalp hasn't remained unscathed this time, but I can't bring myself to deny I enjoyed it. As twisted, reckless, and forbidden as it was, it was also something so euphoric it was catalytic.

Sounds of angry, raised voices float up from downstairs and I tilt my head to listen to the familiarity behind them.

Surely that's not Mr. Marino? He said he would be away for six weeks. It's only been a few.

I throw my legs out of bed and have to grip the nightstand when my head feels woozy and my legs threaten to buckle. I take a deep breath and give myself a minute to regain control of my wayward body.

Casting my eyes around the room, I locate my leggings and T-shirt, then slip them on. I pull on my hoodie to cover the bite marks littering my skin, then throw my hair up into a messy bun.

With a knot in my stomach and a feeling of dread, I reluctantly open my bedroom door and make my way downstairs.

Tommy

I left Jade to sleep in this morning. After last night, her body must be completely drained. The feeling of control over her body, even her orgasm, was sensational and something I can't wait to delve into further with her.

Instead of taking her breakfast in bed, I opted to make her brunch. Setting the breakfast table myself, I realize it's another first for me.

All for the little girl lying in the fluffy pink sheets upstairs. My heart pangs at the thought of how dependent we are on one another. I know it's not healthy, but I refuse to acknowledge it.

My phone vibrates, and I glance down at the screen, noting it's security. While flipping the bacon, I answer. "Sir, I'm just informing you your father is on his way up. He asked for me to call ahead to make sure you're decent."

Confusion swirls in my head, my father? He should be away right now.

"Okay," I mumble, ending the call as I try to figure out why my father would have cut his business trip short. And to ask for me to be decent? Well, that's new. Although to be fair, he's probably found me in so many unfortunate positions over the years it's probably given him nightmares.

The front door opens, so I flick the gas off and move the pan off the stove.

"My office," my father shouts from inside the foyer, making my shoulders harden with rage at his claiming of my office. Like he fucking owns the property.

Slamming down the spatula, I follow his footsteps. Annoyed as fuck that, yet again, he's already ruining what was going to be an amazing day.

I ignore Rafael standing outside my office, a cocky smirk on his face I'm ready to wipe off.

"What the hell do you think you're doing storming into my fucking house like this?" I slam the door behind me for emphasis.

"Your house? Since when?" he scolds.

I inhale deeply, then slowly exhale through my nose. "I think I've earned it, playing my part so you can have Zenya's family business," I snipe back with a knowing glare.

It's the only fucking reason I agreed to marry Zenya, so I could have my own property and a lump sum, enabling me to disconnect from the very people that helped break me.

He at least sits in the visitor's chair, allowing me to sit in my own, where I fucking belong. My fists clench below my desk. The urge to take a hit of something to calm my unraveling nerves and lack of control in this situation burns under my skin. "What brings you back, Father?" I spit, unable to hide the venom behind my tone.

"Jade."

One word. One fucking word and I feel murderous. The use of her name makes me want to tear him apart.

My heart rate increases, and my muscles tense as I bare my teeth. "What the fuck about her?"

"Are you sleeping with her?" His dark eyes hold mine hostage in a silent standoff. "Daddy?" he tacks on, making my head drop in defeat.

When I arranged the setup in the office, I never intended it to go as far as it did. I wanted to taste the forbidden while rubbing his nose in the fact he delivered me my toy to play with. I didn't expect to fall so deeply in love with her I'd drown us both in the depths of an addiction so strong and raw there would be no coming back from it.

I raise my head again, my eyes locking with his in determination. "I love her."

"Love?" He scoffs, and I want nothing more than to pummel his perfect white teeth into the back of his throat. Not for the first time, I despise him.

"You've taken an innocent young girl and corrupted her. Your stepdaughter, no less. You're a fucking addict and I never should have allowed you within six feet of someone so pure as her. You're scum!" he seethes.

I struggle to swallow as his words sink in. He's right in everything he's saying. I am an addict. She is pure and innocent, and I don't deserve her. But I fucking love her. I love her and he will not take her away from me. Panic floods me. Is that what he plans on doing?

"You won't take her from me!" I jump up from my chair, sending it to the floor.

"I can do whatever the hell I want. I'll protect her from the likes of you!" he spits out.

My body threatens to collapse, my heart rate frantic. "Dad, please." He scans me, and a flash of softness inches in, giving me hope, but it's quickly eradicated when his cold eyes bore into mine.

His shoulders relax as he slumps back in his chair,

watching me closely. "I'll give you Justine," he adds, stealing the air I'm breathing as my chest tightens.

His words flip a switch in my brain. Just the sound of her name sends me into a frenzy and I fly across the desk. "You son of a bitch, I knew it. I fucking knew it. You took her from me!"

Firm hands pull me back, and Rafael pins me against his broad chest. "Calm down, brother." I try to shrug him off, but I can't move him.

I've never loathed my father as much as I do in this moment.

As my breathing regulates and I relax against Rafael, I say the words, "I'll do whatever it takes . . ." I admit.

Jade

Rafael's eyes meet mine as my foot moves off the last step. "Go and get in the car, Jade." He nods toward the front door, making me glance there in confusion. "Go on. I'll explain everything shortly." His firm voice leaves no room for argument, so I nod and head toward the open door.

The sound of Tommy's pained voice makes me stop in my tracks with my hand on the door handle. I turn to glance over my shoulder to find Rafael has now gone into the office too.

Taking a deep breath, I tiptoe toward the office door. Keeping my back against the wall to remain undetected, I listen in.

"I'll give you Justine," Mr. Marino says, making my heart free-fall at the sound of her name. My lip quivers and my eyes fill with tears while my heart breaks. He's trading me?

The pain inside my chest manifests, forcing my knees to buckle under the weight of a feeling of pure devastation. My whole world feels like it's crumbling around me.

He's leaving me. Choosing her over me.

Tommy's sharp, scathing voice slices through the air. "You son of a bitch, I knew it. I fucking knew it. You took her from me!" Pain lances my chest at the hurt in his voice, and I struggle to breathe.

Knowing his father is threatening to take me from him, and yet he's still distraught about his ex.

He promised me he was all in. That I was someone special to him. He told me he cared, that I was his to protect. My body shudders as I cling to the wall for support. He used me. He took what he wanted and now he's going to discard me like everyone else does.

A scuffle ensues, but I struggle to gain enough composure to care. I push off the wall, my mind and heart shattered and my pulse racing so hard I feel light-headed. Like I'm floating in a sea of misery. Drowning, in fact. And there's no one there to save me.

"I'll do whatever it takes . . ."

It's all I hear as I walk toward the door, swiping away the lone tear that cascades down my face and onto the floor.

I step outside and into a future without Tommy, without my daddy.

Chapter Nineteen

Four months later . . .

Tommy

I glance up at my father's mansion. When I left rehab last week, I headed home first and put things in place for when I returned. When we return. I've spent the last fourteen weeks dreaming of this day, of her.

Things need to be different this time around. I will do things right. I will be the man she deserves if she'll allow me, of course.

Fuck that, I'm taking her whether she's ready or not. After all, I have an agreement with my father. She's mine.

When I screamed, "I'll do whatever it takes. I'm keeping her," darting my arm out to grip his tie, turning his face a dark shade of red, he saw the look of fierce determination behind my eyes. The sincerity in my tone left no room for argument.

In that moment, I didn't care they'd taken Justine away from me. All I cared about was Jade.

My father tilted his head toward my chair for me to take a seat, and with a push of encouragement that set my teeth on edge from Rafael, I finally picked up my chair and slumped my reluctant ass back down.

"So, let's get this straight"—he pointed at me—"you don't want to know where Justine is?"

I worked my jaw from side to side. Was he this stupid? "No. She's not important here," I spat out.

His thick eyebrows furrowed, and he reared back. "Why not?"

"Because she doesn't matter anymore." I shook my head. "The only person that matters to me is Jade. I love her."

My father watched me closely as my heart hammered dangerously against my chest, threatening to burst at any second.

He sighed heavily as he rested back in his chair. "I offered Justine an out." He admitted, making my ears prick up and my hands ball into fists. I knew it. "I offered her three hundred thousand dollars and a new identity to leave your ass, and the girl didn't bat an eye. She left." He flicked his finger as though emphasizing how easy it was to get rid of her.

I swallowed back the lump in my throat. All those wasted years pining after a girl that fucked me over. Years wasted. I felt a deep ache in my chest when I considered the time I missed out with family, at gatherings and holidays, all due to her betrayal when I so easily blamed them for scaring her away.

Would I have listened if they tried to explain before now? Probably not. I was too deep in my loathing to listen. Needing someone to blame, they became the easy target. I did, after all, know they had something to do with it.

"I set up Jenna and sent Rafael over here to check on Jade. When he reported back confirming my suspicions of your relationship, I knew I had to step in." My pulse raced as he spoke. "And when I heard that you knocked Jenna back, I knew there was more to your relationship with Jade. Hoped there was more to it. You never turned down easy pussy before now."

My eyes darted toward his in shock. Hoped?

"She'll make the perfect wife for you, Tommy."

Had he really set this up? Had he brought my step-daughter into my lair with the expectations of it becoming more?

"Of course, I'd hoped you'd fall in love with her over time, not while she's at such a tender age." He clucked his tongue in disapproval. "Still, eighteen is the Mafia way of life." He shrugged. Leaning over my desk, his menacing eyes met with mine. "Now, if you're serious about this. You have some work to do, son." The glint in his eyes was full of promise and, if I'm not mistaken, pride too.

I nodded in agreement, prepared to do whatever it took to keep my girl and, in the process, get my life back on track.

Taking a deep breath, I open the mansion door with a new sense of purpose in mind. My future.

Our future.

I stride through the foyer and head straight toward the kitchen. Having heard from my father about how much time she's enjoyed spending there, I intend on building her a bakery of her own if she wishes.

Swinging open the kitchen door, I'm stunned to silence when her emerald gaze meets mine. She's beauty personified. My blood pumps thicker as the air around us seems to still, holding us in a trance. My whole body freezes, captivated by her stare, with only the heavy thud of my heart filling the space between us.

Jade licks her bottom lip, and I watch in rapture as her tongue flicks out to gather the dusting of frosting from the corner of her mouth. The action makes my fingers itch to touch her.

"Hello, little girl." Using her nickname makes my cock twitch against my slacks. How I've fucking longed to use it.

Her chest rises rapidly, her eyes fill with tears, and when her lip quivers, my heart skips a beat. Then she clears her throat and straightens her shoulders, raising her chin with an air of confidence that I'm proud of. "What do you want?" she bites out. Annoyed at my surprising presence.

My voice clogs, and my words come out in a gentle whisper, "You. Just you, Jade."

I don't miss the tremor that takes over her body at the use of her name. Or maybe it's because I'm admitting I want her.

She turns her head to the side as though unable to look at me, the movement causing my stomach to sink.

"What about Justine?" Her voice comes out as a croak laced with hurt.

Her hand tightens on the spoon she's holding as my mind fights the cloud of confusion behind her words.

"Justine?" I question, more to myself than her.

"Is that where you think I've been?"

My blood turns to anger. It simmers rapidly as it boils toward the surface of my skin, threatening to seep through.

Have they not told her where I've been? How I've worked so fucking hard at creating a better version of me. For her.

"They didn't tell you?" I grit out. Of course, they didn't. They thought I'd fail. Guilt stabs me in the chest at how much pain I've caused. How little my own family thought of me.

Her eyes finally meet mine. The look of hurt marring her features makes me want to lash out, but I rein it in. To protect her. I'd do anything for her. Anything.

"Tell me what?"

"I entered rehab voluntarily." My throat is suddenly dry, but I push past it. "I went to rehab so I can be the best person for you."

When her eyes soften, I want nothing more than to scoop her into my arms and shower her with delicate kisses while whispering thoughts of my gratitude to her. Telling her how brave she's been while I've been gone, but Daddy's home now. Daddy will take care of her. My cock pulsates. It's been too fucking long since I had her. Since her touch.

"What about . . ." Her voice trails off as though deep in thought. Mulling over my words, perhaps.

I shake my head. "I told you no one else would exist. Not when I have you. You're my cure, little girl. My reason for living. Am I your reason, too?"

She shakes her head, making my head fall forward in defeat, my shoulders slump and my heart stutters. I feel like the world is crashing down around me as I stand frozen to the spot with my heart constricting from her action.

What I've been hoping would be a happy reunion will soon turn into protests when I whisk her away without her consent. Because I refuse to leave here without her.

I don't care what anyone says. She's mine.

"You're my addiction, Tommy. And I'm your cure. I think that's the best kind of obsession. Don't you?"

My head snaps up and I move to step forward, but she holds her hand up to stop me. I freeze, knowing what she will say is going to hurt. The look of apprehension and seriousness on her face says it all. She doesn't think we're right for one another. But I'll do everything in my power to change her mind.

"I've something to confess." Her cheeks pinken on her admittance.

My chest tightens, and my pulse quickens. Is it that fucker, Darryl? I'll kill him. I'll kill him and fuck her in his blood too.

Slowly, she unties her apron, her fingers trembling, and then she steps out from behind the counter.

My gaze roams down her hot little body and comes to a still at her stomach, where a small bump sits tauntingly. Emotion clogs in my throat and I lick my dry lips, struggling to form the words. "You're . . . you're pregnant?"

"I am." She nibbles on her bottom lip and wrings her hands in front of her before settling them on the swell of her stomach, where our baby lies.

My whole body vibrates with excitement, every cell in me alive.

They're fucking mine!

I stride forward without thinking. Her mouth falls open in shock while mine breaks out into an enormous smile encompassing my face. Tenderly, I place my hand on her small bump and revel in her body swaying against mine as if in shock at my action.

Dropping kisses of gratitude on her head and breathing in her scent, my body swells with pride, with a love that is simply indescribable.

Feeling so fucking grateful, so lucky to have my girl in my life, and now our baby too.

I turn her to face me, taking my hands and placing them on either side of her face. My eyes lock onto her teary ones. "I love you, little girl."

She blinks away the tears and her lip quivers. "I love you too."

Our lips collide and sparks ignite as I close my eyes and embrace her and our future.

A cure for the perfect addiction.

Chapter Twenty

Jade

All that time, Tommy had been gone, and not one of them breathed a word about his whereabouts. Not once.

I believed he had run off into the sunset with his ex when, in reality, he was working on himself for me, for us.

I guess it was their way of protecting me. Doubting his ability to follow through and combat his demons.

But they doubted his strength and our love for one another.

When I discovered I was pregnant a few weeks after he left, Mr. Marino was surprisingly sympathetic, considering I was having a baby out of wedlock, with his son, no less.

He allowed me to continue working at the local bakery while undertaking cooking classes, telling me it was a good move to make to become a perfect housewife and mother. Something until now I hadn't thought much of.

Maybe this was his hope all along?

"I really need to fuck you now, little girl," Tommy pants

as he pulls his lips from mine. He grinds his hard cock against me, causing wetness to pool in my panties.

"Yes, yes please," I breathe out as he steals kisses, lifting my dress around my waist. "My room." I tap his shoulder. "Take me to my room."

He nods against my neck, then he sinks his teeth into the skin with a groan while I tackle tugging his belt open. Lifting me, I wrap my legs around him as he walks us up the stairs.

"Second door. On the right," I pant as our tongues fight desperately against one another's.

"Mmm, fuck, you taste so good." He pulls back as he kicks open my door. "Missed you so damn much." Then he pushes it shut with his ass.

Gently, he lowers me onto the bed, then tears his shirt from his chest, his eyes trained on me as I pull my dress over my head, exposing my white bra and lace panties. Heat travels over my body with the hungry look in his eyes; he's devouring me. His body is rigid, and the veins protruding across his chest show me he's restraining himself.

Those olive abs of his are on full display, and I want nothing more than to run my tongue along them, feeling every ridge and ripple as I do.

"Fuck, little girl." His heavy eyes flash with desire, the lust oozing from them giving me the confidence to peel my bra from my body and slip my panties down my legs as he remains frozen on the spot.

Sitting up on my elbows, I widen my legs, giving him the perfect view of my bare pussy, and move my finger to lazily stroke over my swollen clit. My arousal coats my digit as I repeat the motion, this time slipping inside my pussy hole and earning a low growl from him.

"Fuck." He snaps out of his trance, kicking his socks and

shoes off at rapid speed and dropping his pants and boxers in one swoop, revealing his thick, solid cock with precum dripping from the bulging head.

He tugs it tightly a few times and hisses through his teeth at the contact. "Please, Daddy," I beg. "I need you to fill me."

"Fuck. Yes." He crawls onto the bed. "Only Daddy can fuck this little pussy." He drags his fingers over my slit and down into my wetness. A moan slips from my lips when he rubs his finger against mine, encouraging me. We both push our fingers inside me, and his eyes flicker between my pussy and my face as though he's scared of missing out on something. I buck against him with need, and he lets out a low chuckle. Then he positions himself between my legs, with his eyes transfixed on my fingers, when he withdraws his own.

"Only Daddy can fill you, right, little girl?" He tacks on while watching my finger play.

"Yes, only you. Only ever you." I buck my hips up again.

"Good girl, keep playing with your little cunt while Daddy fills you." He strokes his cock up and down my slit, nudging at my entrance with each downstroke as I push up against him, making his lips tip up at my response.

"Fuck. You're needy, little girl."

"So needy," I agree. I can't even lie about how desperate I am for him. My hormones have been creating havoc with me, making me crave the very man that broke my heart.

"Daddy likes watching you play." His cock jerks at his words, making me moan.

He trails a hand over the small swell of my stomach. "We're having a baby, little girl."

"Yes, Daddy."

"Daddy filled you good, didn't he?" His teeth latch on to my neck while his hand roams to my tits, kneading them and tugging on my sensitive nipples. "I can't wait to watch these fill with milk for me."

"Mm," I moan at his words and the promise of his touch, wetness pooling from my pussy.

"They're for the baby."

His eyes snap back up to mine. "They're mine."

My mouth falls open in shock at his possessiveness. "But Daddy can share," he adds with a smirk.

I whimper when the head of his cock teases my entrance once again. "Please, Daddy, I need you."

"Good girl." He pulls his hips back and slams inside me, making me gasp in surprise at the sudden action. His cock stretches me, filling me all in one. The bite of pain behind the intrusion, with the burst of pleasure from his tongue caressing my nipple, sends a sudden burst of fulfillment through me.

"Fuck," he grinds out, slamming into me again when he feels my body clench around him.

"Daddy!" I scream as my body convulses, locking up tight, drawing him in farther.

The fact I orgasmed so quickly shows how needy I am, how desperately I've longed for his touch.

"Fuck, that's it. Come on Daddy's thick cock." He continues pounding into me, and my nails dig into his flesh, marking him eagerly.

"Daddy's little slut is filled with a baby, isn't she?" His hand once again touches my bump as a wave of arousal seeps from my body. "Fuck, Daddy put a baby in here, didn't he?" His filthy words and the sparks of electricity with each graze of our skin make vibrations flow through me.

His hips snap forward at a brutal pace while I cling to his back as he slams inside me ferally.

The power behind his thick body against my small one leaves me as a vessel for his ship, and he surges inside me, building another tidal wave of arousal. His cock thickens and the tsunami crashes through us, sending me spiraling through a wave of never-ending pleasure.

"Fuck. Fuck. Fuck," he chants from above me, but it's background noise as my spine arches, my eyes roll back, and my lips part.

A rush of wetness spills from me, but I can barely move to witness it, my whole body dazed at the intensity of my orgasm.

He withdraws from me, then holds my legs open.

I lift my head slightly to see him. He watches the cum drip from my pussy, then uses two fingers to stroke it down toward my ass.

My eyes widen as he slips them inside, the sharpness of it making me wince, then he slides them deeper. I fidget uncomfortably against him, but his grip tightens on my leg, warning me to allow him to use me. "Shh, be a good girl and lie there. Daddy's going to fuck this ass now, little girl."

My heart hammers as he scissors his fingers inside me, as my ass opens for him. "Daddy needs all your holes." Then he pulls his fingers out and replaces them with the tip of his cock.

"This might hurt, little girl. But you're going to be brave and let Daddy take your ass." His eyes lock with mine. The cords of his muscled chest stretch as though restraining himself before I gift him a nod and he slowly pushes past the tight, muscled barrier.

"Please, I need—" I glance down toward my clit in question, asking him for some reprieve, for his approval if my fingers were to touch it and help me push past the pain and into the pleasure.

"No," he chides, shaking his head. "No, you're going to feel Daddy take you here like I took your pussy. Daddy's going to stretch this tight little hole wide open. Be a good girl and let Daddy take you," he pants, his face contorting in euphoria. "Let Daddy stretch this little ass wide for his big cock." He pushes in a little farther, then, without warning, he sears through my tender flesh, deep into my ass, making me scream in pain as a sharp burn unleashes inside me. "Good fucking girl." He pulls back, then snaps his hips sharply forward as though angry. "Good fucking girl," he repeats, then bites into the side of his mouth when he pulls out and slams back in again. While one hand roams over the swell of our baby, he fucks my ass feverishly.

"Daddy," I whimper.

"Fucking take it. Take my cock in your ass." He slams inside me again, and I have no choice but to take it.

All of it.

Every thick inch makes me feel like he's tearing me apart. But I wouldn't change it for the world.

I love him. I love his brutality, his filthy, uncontrollable obsession with me.

So, when his body tightens and his cock thickens, allowing the ropes of his cum to spill into my ass, I relish it. Feeling treasured and perplexed, finally feeling loved.

Tommy

After fucking my girl into oblivion, I lift her into my arms and carry her into the bathtub. While I'm not thrilled about washing away my cum, I can admit she needs some tender care, and I'll always be the man to do it.

She rests against my chest while my hands palm her small bump. I've never felt so fiercely protective over anyone before.

"Has everything been okay so far with the pregnancy?" She tilts her head to face me.

"Yes. They didn't tell you about it, then?" She bites into her lip, making me groan at the back of my throat.

"No." I drag a hand through my hair. "Unfortunately, I think them doing that was for the best. I think that was the right decision by my father."

Her eyes flash with hurt, forcing me to elaborate. "I'd have been straight out of rehab, barging in here and taking you home." I chuckle as her shoulders relax, and I gift her neck with a gentle kiss.

When her fingers trail over my tattoos, it's me that melts against her touch.

"He did right," she agrees. "You needed to get stronger. For both of us."

My hands press gently on her bump. "For both of you." Our lips meet.

"Marry me?" I ask, pulling back to stare into her emerald eyes.

Air leaves her lips in surprise before they tip up into a serene smile, where she nibbles on her lip.

"Say yes," I coax, my gaze drilling into hers, leaving her no choice but to comply.

"Yes, Daddy." She grins back at me.

"Good girl." Her lips find mine as she turns to straddle me, her sore ass forgotten when I grip her ass cheeks in the palms of my hands and line up my cock before slamming her down, making her lips part.

"I love you, little girl."

"I love you too, Daddy."

Chapter Twenty-One

Jade

Tommy's grin encompasses his face as he opens the door to my bedroom, then moves aside, allowing me to step inside.

The frilly pink bedding is gone, and in its place are soft shades of green and white-painted walls. I stroke my hand over the silk bed linen, feeling like an awakening has taken place.

"Will this be your room now too?" I turn and face him.

His broad shoulders fill out his black shirt, the muscles behind them straining against the material, making me clench my legs with need.

While being away from me, he's been working out and what was once a chiseled body is now homage to a rock-solid machine.

"Of course." He pushes off the door and walks toward me. "Although I'm kind of going to miss the frilly pink shit." His lips quirk up at the side. "It added to the element of taboo, don't you think?" He raises an eyebrow, making me chuckle.

I slide my dress down my shoulders, letting it pool at my feet, earning a hiss from Tommy. "You mean the element where I'm your stepdaughter and you creep into my room, making me take your cock?"

His pupils flare with need, then he shakes his head. "There's no creeping, little girl. Daddy storms into your room and tells you to kneel while he fucks your mouth so hard you can't speak."

I drop to my knees, and he steps closer, unbuckling his belt. Then I slide his zipper down, letting him pull his thick, hard cock from his slacks. The vein protrudes on the side, and I itch to lick it. When his tattooed hands tug his boxers below his balls, I look up into his heady stare. "Lick my balls, little girl. Lick my balls and work that tongue over my thick cock." I do as he asks, lowering my gaze to concentrate on his sack. I follow the veins, rolling my tongue over the delicate skin and delighting in it, making his hips thrust in approval. His hand finds my hair. Those tattooed fingers grip it so roughly it stings, hurts even.

"Fuck yeah. Like that," he pants.

I work my way up his solid shaft, the velvety feel beneath my tongue an aphrodisiac, sending bolts of pleasure down my spine and pooling between my legs.

"Mm, good little slut. Take Daddy's cock in your naughty little mouth." I glance up to find him staring down at me, those dark orbs of his heavy and full of want and his lips parted in awe. I work my tongue up and over the tip, then suck the head into my mouth, dipping my tongue into the slit. He grunts, thrusting up into me, "Such a good girl. Get it nice and wet."

Trying my best to swallow him, I bob my head down his

cock. "Fuck, yes. Like that," he breathes out through gritted teeth. "Daddy's going to fuck this mouth now. Are you ready for me, little girl?"

My eyes meet his and I try to mumble a "yes," but it comes out garbled, making him chuckle sadistically. Without further warning, he grips my head tighter, pushing me flush against his groin. My hands grip his thighs as I try and pull back, but he doesn't allow it. Instead, I'm forced to splutter and try to gasp for air, but he ignores me, plunging his length deep into my throat. Choking around him, I'm unable to take it all, but he doesn't relent as saliva drips from my mouth and tears stream down my face. He holds my head in his palms and fucks me hard, uncaring of my protests and desperation to get air. I panic, trying relentlessly to breathe through my nose as spittle drips onto the floor.

Yet when he begins talking in his deliciously filthy voice, I relax and accept my fate as a hole to fill his cock and ultimately accept his cum. "Fuck, you're incredible, little girl. A perfect wet hole for Daddy's cock." He pulls out, making me gasp for air, before slamming back inside without giving me a chance to breathe it in. "That's it, choke on it. Choke on Daddy's thick cock, you little slut."

My throat hurts with the force of his thrusts, but he doesn't relent. He holds my head in a viselike grip, using it as he sees fit. Fucking it. "Goddamn, little girl." His cock swells at the back of my throat, and when I glance up, his eyes roll in ecstasy. "Oh fuck, you're making Daddy come. Fuck." His warm cum splashes in my throat before I swallow him down.

Tommy stumbles slightly at the force and has to apply pressure to the back of my head to stay in place. His labored breaths slowly regulate to a steady pace as he slips his cock from me.

"You've no idea how fucking beautiful you look right now." The backs of his fingers graze my cheek lovingly.

"Mine," he breathes out as our eyes lock.

"Yours," I reply, knowing that for the rest of our lives, I will always be the cure to his addiction.

Epilogue

Five Months Later . . .

Jade

Faith nuzzles against my breast as she nurses from me. I stroke over her dark locks, loving the feel of her silky hair between my fingers. When I gave birth to Faith, it was the most incredible day of my life. Tommy was everything I needed him to be: supportive, loving, and powerful. I now see a side of him I hadn't seen before; he's controlled and determined to be the perfect father to our daughter while remaining my daddy in the bedroom. Faith was the perfect name for our little girl because I have every ounce of faith in him that he will continue to do us proud.

He's been running his father's clubs, and I'm in awe at the way he's transformed himself for us. He says I'm his new addiction, and I couldn't be more grateful.

The bedroom door creaks open, and Tommy's eyes roam over me and then fill with an unadulterated love when they lock onto our daughter, who's nursing. I glance at the clock and see it's almost five a.m. He's late and must be exhausted.

My gaze never leaves his as he slowly peels his clothes from his sculpted body, making heat travel over my own.

I glance down at Faith, wishing her to hurry with her feeding while flicking my eyes over to Tommy. His heavy cock is standing tall as he pulls back the sheets and slides inside. His palm meets my stomach, and he tugs me closer while using his other hand to prop himself up on his elbow and rest his head against his palm, watching me feed her.

"Is she saving some milk for Daddy?" He crooks his eyebrow in question.

I want to whimper at his words but refrain from doing so in our daughter's presence. Instead, I let her finish feeding before gently removing her from my breast. "Do you want me to take her from you?"

"No, I can manage." I smile back at Tommy while I adjust my nightie into place and maneuver the sheets to lift her into her crib beside the bed, placing a kiss on her fore-head. I smile at the frown forming on her sleepy face.

I slink back beneath the sheets, and before my head touches my pillow, Tommy has a nightie strap down to expose my breast to him.

I know what he wants. He wants my milk too. He wants every part of me.

So I lay my head against the pillow and hold my swollen breast up for him to take. A growl leaves his throat, the sound so feral a whoosh of air escapes my lungs as his mouth finds my nipple roughly.

Tommy sucks hard, making milk surge into his mouth. My fingers tangle in his hair as I hold him into place, loving the bite of pain when his teeth graze the tips, then the hard suckle that follows to release my pleasure. "Oh god, Daddy."

"Mmm." His vibrations send flurries of exhilaration to my pussy. "You like Daddy feeding from you, don't you?" The grip on my breast feels bruising as his mouth devours me, and his body rocks back and forth, thrusting his hard cock against me, proving he's losing control.

Before I know what's happening, he pulls away abruptly and straddles my body. His eyes are wild, his body tense, but I know what he wants. Tommy is obsessed with milk play. I push my tits together for him, letting him situate himself between my breasts. "Squeeze your milk out." His tone is clipped and full of darkness, letting me know he will be brutal with my body.

I do as he commands, squeezing my nipples to allow the flow of my warm milk over his solid cock. He hisses between his teeth. "That's it, wet Daddy's cock with your milk, baby girl." He begins to thrust his hips as my milk flows between us while he cages me in with his hands on either side of my pillow.

Watching his mouth fall open in ecstasy, my pussy drips with a desperate need to please him. "Good girl. Good little slut for Daddy."

He surges forward. "Open that mouth, let Daddy feed you."

His body rocks back and forth, back and forth. Fucking my tits, the weight of his body pins me down, giving me no choice but for him to use me like a doll. I open my mouth willingly for him, but when I expect the tip of his cock to push past my lips, he surprises me and moves his hands to my throat, bends his head, and spits into my mouth. "That's it, little slut. Let Daddy use you." His body powers against me, thrusting against my tits. Sweat coats his forehead like a second skin, and his dark locks fall into his eyes, and I've never seen him look so gorgeous, dark, and deranged, and my pussy clenches at the thought of the dangerous combination. Truly intoxicating.

"Fuck, you drip so well for me. Leave that mouth open. Let Daddy use his beautiful little slut." He spits into my mouth again, and his eyes roll in rapture when my tits release an influx of milk around him.

"Fuckkkk." He grips my throat with both hands, choking me, making me gasp in frantic panic. Tommy's eyes flare on the action. "Leave your fucking mouth open. Let me fill what's mine." The weight of his body on me and the pressure on my pulse points have my vision darkening. I'm vaguely aware of my chest filling with warm heat as my husband coats me in his essence.

I drift back down to earth to feel him stretching my pussy wide. With my chest now coated in his cum, I'm gasping for breath, relishing in his pleasure, bathing in it.

"My beautiful addiction. My beautiful little girl."

I palm my breasts, mixing my milk with his cum, embracing the flare of his pupils when I do so.

"Yours, Daddy. All yours."

THE END

MORE DADDY?

Daddy's Addiction will be part of a new stand-alone series.

You can order Rafael and Ellie's story here: **Daddy's Possession.**

Rocco's story is available for preorder here: **Daddy's Manipulation**

Also by BJ Alpha

Born Series

Born Reckless

The Brutal Duet

Hidden In Brutal Devotion

Love In Brutal Devotion

The Brutal Duet Part Two

Brutal Secrets

Brutal Lies

STORM ENTERPRISES

SHAW Book 1

TATE Book 2

Secrets and Lies Series

CAL Book 1

CON Book 2

FINN Book 3

BREN Book 4

OSCAR Book 5

CON'S WEDDING NOVELLA

VEILED IN Series

VEILED IN HATE

Acknowledgments

**Tee the lady that started it all for me.
Thank you, thank you, thank you!**

I must start with where it all began, TL Swan. When I started reading your books, I never realized I was in a place I needed pulling out of. Your stories brought me back to myself.

With your constant support and the network created as 'Cygnet Inkers' I was able to create something I never realized was possible, I genuinely thought I'd had my day. You made me realize tomorrow is just the beginning.

**To Kate,
Thank you for letting me continuously bounce
ideas off of you, any time of the day, night…
Scrap that every hour, minute, second.
Your enthusiasm is infectious, and you always
seem to know when I need it the most.
Can you believe the most insane person I know,
actually keeps me sane.
Thank you.**

A special mention to my friends for your continual support,
Lilibet, Emma, Libby, Jaclyn, Tash and Marie.

ARC Team

To my ARC readers thank you.
I'm incredibly lucky to have you as part of my team. I
appreciate you. Your videos, messages, posts, reviews.
Thank you.

To my world.

My boys, I hope you never read this.

To my hubby, the J in my BJ.

Thank you for being you. Love you trillions.

About the Author

BJ Alpha lives in the UK with her hubby, two teenage sons and three fur babies.
She loves to write and read about hot, alpha males and feisty females.

Follow BJ on her social media pages:
Facebook: BJ Alpha
My readers group: BJ's Reckless Readers
Instagram: BJ Alpha

And don't forget to sign up to BJ's Newsletter for exclusive information and competitions. Newsletter sign up.

www.ingramcontent.com/pod-product-compliance
Lightning Source LLC
Chambersburg PA
CBHW070506120726
47910CB00003B/1141